into the valley

into
the
valley

Ruth Galm

SOHO

Published by
Soho Press, Inc.
853 Broadway
New York, NY 10003

Library of Congress Cataloging-in-Publication Data

Galm, Ruth
Into the valley / Ruth Galm.

ISBN 978-1-61695-509-0
eISBN 978-1-61695-510-6

1. Women—Fiction. 2. Conflict of generations—Fiction.
3. Psychological fiction. I. Title.
PS3607.A423I58 2015

813'.6—dc23   2015009876

Interior design by Janine Agro, Soho Press, Inc.

Printed in the United States of America

10 9 8 7 6 5 4 3 2 1

For Paul

i.

SHE TOOK THE FORGED CHECK to the bank and cashed it.
From there, she walked to the drugstore. She bought tampons
and a candy bar (she did not in that moment think of what else
she might need) and coiled the rest of the bills in a roll in her
bra strap because it did not feel right to have them in her purse.
It was a strange bulge at her shoulder, papery and hard, but
the sheath was loose enough to hide it. She rode the bus
over the hill to her apartment and waited at the corner for
the landlady to leave for her daily groceries. It was a basement apartment with no direct light and a dank stone smell no
matter what carpets and furniture and ceramic vases of lilies
B. had tried to add to it. A small kitchenette had been built in
the corner around a dump sink, and she had added a Formica
table with two chairs, but the corner still radiated a metallic

damp smell. There was a small room next to the bathroom that she'd planned to use as a study or a hobby room, but her only hobby was reading and it made the carsickness worse to read in that cramped space with no natural light, so she left it empty. She knew, in the end, none of it amounted to anything people wanted to hear about in conversation.

In a vinyl bag she gathered a few dresses, underwear, a nightgown, alongside her ostrich-skin purse. She went to her dresser and drew out the velvet box with the diamond brooch she had not touched in two years. When she had everything, she took the bus to a car lot on Van Ness. She had seen the Mustang for sale for months, glittering blue in the bright fog-bleached light, the elongated trunk like the snout of an alligator, she thought, and the body just as slinky and low to the ground. It was a V-8 engine, the salesman warned her. "You don't know what kind of power an engine like that has. Out of nowhere, you're flying." He tried to sell her a Chevrolet, what he called a "more appropriate" car, or a Chrysler, a car "more for someone your type," but she excused herself to the ladies' room and extracted the exact amount for the Mustang from the largest bills in the bra strap.

She got behind the wheel and backed out self-consciously as the salesman watched. The steering wheel was large in front of her, hard thin metal and tight plastic coating. The engine jumped at a touch to the gas. As she made her way carefully out of the car lot onto Van Ness, she did not even think of it as leaving, only "going away." She drove through the city and east across the bridge and wanted simply to put the relentless appeal of the water behind her. The freeway skirted green piney hills dotted with cottages. She imagined them filled one by one with women, mothers and housewives, and she wondered very genuinely how they filled their days, whether they arranged to come down and buy vegetables and attend luncheons or preferred to stay in the cottages as long as they could. She switched on the radio. A song was playing that had played at her first high school dance, and she remembered the peach satin dress and the perfume her mother dabbed at her wrists and the Brylcreemed boy, and for a moment she was taken with the same abstract hopefulness she'd had that night. That something she'd been waiting for would arrive and overtake her. But when the song ended, a commercial jangled on and she found only rock and roll on the next two stations, until finally she flicked the radio off and listened instead to the asphalt breaks beneath her.

She left the green mountains and followed the freeway along the bay, the water seeming never to recede, snaking ever inland. Finally she came to another, smaller bridge and there was no water after that. She felt an inexplicable relief. There were a few houses on the side of the freeway and a roadside nightclub with unlit neon palm trees on its roof, and then suddenly she was in the "golden" hills. They were a sere, sad blond. As the Mustang took the grade through the treeless, waterless land, she did not think of the money at her shoulder or the possessions she'd left behind or her secretarial job at the law firm to which she would not return. When she reached the top of the hill, she took her foot off the gas and coasted downward to the flat valley below and thought of nothing.

.

ii.

THE TELLER HAD ASKED HER, glancing at the ostrich-skin purse, if she liked the new tapestry handbags. "They're like something out of Mary Poppins," B. had said. The teller nodded in agreement. She had beautifully applied shimmer eye shadow. She counted the bills out sharply and brushed back a lock of washed-and-set hair. The first bank B. would never forget because of these details and because of the first flush of expansive coolness. The lines and the marble and the calm suffusing her. She had smiled at the soignée teller and breathed without spinning and pocketed three thousand stolen dollars.

iii.

"DID YOU LIKE THE NEW salon? Do you have a date this week?"

Her last conversation with her mother had been exactly like the others.

"I've decided, by the way, that I really prefer the pearlescents for manicures."

Underneath, the carsickness had drummed as though to seam apart her skull. She answered the questions by rote, and through the drumming an indistinct thought pulsed, as blurred and throbbing as the pain: There must be another conversation they were meant to have. Some other point to which they could apply their exchange.

"Are you not feeling well?" her mother asked.

"No."

"Be sure to take some air. It'll brighten your skin."

And with that, B. had hung up the phone.

iv.

SHE ROLLED DOWN HER WINDOW. Heat blasted her cheek. She exited the freeway and took a road next to some railroad tracks, rusted boxcars abandoned in a long chain.

The wind whipped through the interior, smelling of vinyl and exhaust. She stepped on the gas.

The irony was that she felt the carsickness less in the car. The irony was that the carsickness had nothing to do with actually being in one.

She drove past a lone barn newly painted white and a couple of one- and two-room shacks next to the road, canted picket fences lost in tall grass, dirty old trucks in the driveways. She passed the brown skeleton of a structure, not burned but somehow bared to its dark wooden bones, ringed by NO TRES-PASSING signs on trees all around. It looked to her in its openness like an ancient place of worship, and she felt a brief urge to stop and sit inside its timbers, but she drove on. A sign read 60 MILES TO SACRAMENTO.

She could go see the capitol. She knew dimly that she would not. She knew dimly that she would never go near another city again.

v.

THE VALLEY WAS BECAUSE OF the man on the bus. She tried always to smile at people in public as her mother had taught her, to look polite and receptive, and they mistook this for an invitation to unburden themselves, when in fact she did not really even want to talk. When he found out she was from the East, the man told her about the long table of land just beyond the mountains and bay. "Nothing happens there. Not one thing." That's why, he explained, the easterners never even knew about it. "No pretty scenes, no trees. Just flat. I won't go back in a million years." She could see in the man's features—he was young with large pores glazed in oil and jagged purple veins on his eyelids—something strained and unbalanced. His eyes blazed. He began to mumble. "But I'm safe here, I really am." B. listened politely for a few more seconds, then got off the bus two stops before her own.

And yet, since the encounter, her thoughts had often drifted to this valley. She imagined that in this long unvarying plane, all the contradictions of the city might fall away. That its bareness would reveal something, provide an answer she had failed to acquire. A place of unvarnished truth to which she must go.

Because it was no longer just the dirty young people in the city who disturbed her. In the restroom at I. Magnin recently, she'd encountered a mother and her teenage daughter. The girl with clear breasts and long legs, as tall as the woman. But the daughter was trying to pull her skirt off. "I'm not sure I want to be wearing it all day," she said. "What if I get cold? What will I do?" The mother hushing and soothing her, keeping the girl's hands from the skirt while the girl shuddered. B. washed herself quickly, but the mother looked straight at her, voice harried: "She's only ten. She looks older, but she's only ten." B. had nodded and run out.

vi.

WHAT SHE HAD NOT THOUGHT through were the logistics. She had not considered how in this tabula rasa she would find the banks. This new state of affairs, this new exigency, she did not question. She only knew she would find them.

vii.

SHE HAD RENAMED HERSELF "B." after college. She thought that was the beginning of the problem: she'd never felt like a Beverly, never known what a Beverly should want to do. The singsong syllables and the lift at the end like a promise made without her agreement, disorienting her. So she'd erased it. People heard it as "Bea," and that was fine with her. As long as she could think of herself as B., something opened up, went blank in a way she could tolerate.

For a time.

viii.

THE PAPER SLIDING ACROSS MARBLE. The tellers' anodyne voices.

Later it was all spoiled. By the glint of the knife, the blood, the expression on Daughtry's face as she drove away.

But by then it no longer mattered.

ix.

"BECAUSE YOU'RE A GOOD GIRL, they'll like you. Because you look normal and you act normal and you've done up your hair and you've walked in the right way, with class, you're gonna fool them blind.

"Because I've always told you: you're a good, classy girl and that won't ever change."

1.

THE CAR WAS LOW ON gas. She had not checked the gauge before leaving the lot and she flushed at the thought of the salesman making a joke of her. (No, she had not wanted a Chevy or a Chrysler. She knew this instinctively, although she might only have been able to say it was the look of the car. Something strong and sharp in the Mustang that pared it down to a single purpose, an inarguable direction. She'd never considered owning a car before. The subways and elevateds in the East had obviated any need, and perhaps, more importantly, owning her own car had seemed somehow unseemly. The women in advertisements lounged around cars in feather boas in the company of tuxedoed dates or carted bags of groceries to the back of a station wagon. And so she had tried to put the thought out of her mind, like some lurid afternoon fantasy, but the empirical beauty of the Mustang had stayed with her, and the car was the first thing she thought of after the check.)

There were no buildings in sight. The July heat made her arms and back sweat, moistening and drying and moistening again. Her left arm turned red in the sun. The city never got hot. Even on the warmest days, she shivered, her toes chilled. She wetted her dry lips and tried to put the anxiety about the gas out of her mind, and when she began to see the first rows of fruit trees, she turned into a dirt lane and parked.

Hundreds of peach trees. She rolled down her stockings and took off the bone-colored heels. The ground was dry and hard, the trees not high but in full leaf, crammed with hard orange peaches. She walked until she found a good spot to sit down. The tree was uncomfortable to lean against and the branches too low, so she lay all the way down on her back and tried to relax. A hot day in her childhood, she had snuck into a vacant lot and lay hidden and cooled in the overgrown grass, among the sounds of cars and birds and cicadas. She'd been convinced of the fact she was erased from the world and breathed easy and fallen asleep. She could not remember another day like that since.

She ate her candy bar, moving her tongue along her teeth for the chocolate and clumps of coconut, and pondered the sky through the peaches. Her throat was dry. She had nothing to drink. It was somewhere after one o'clock on a Tuesday and no cars passed. She tried to keep lying as she had in the vacant lot those years ago but the dirt was hard, and she was not hidden, and eventually she went back to the car and drove on.

She passed a horse corral. No people seemed to be around anywhere. The sun blazed on the animals, their heads bent under the heat, their bodies a liquid brown. They seemed to B., in their unconsciousness, in a state of total equanimity. After the horses came a stretch of dry, uncultivated land and then finally there was a gas station.

She filled up and went to the small bathroom at the back of the building. She saw that the whole back of her dress was dirty. The ivory had not been a wise decision, not for driving or sitting in the dirt, not for the second day of her period. Her underwear had spots of blood where her tampon bled through. She never paid enough attention to when her period might arrive and so was never prepared. And when it did come she seemed, irrationally, to disbelieve that it could require more than one or two tampons. That the blood would run on and on for so many days. She was invariably left with soiled underwear and bloody fingers. She took out the tampon and put another in and folded toilet paper over the blood spots. She went inside the store to pay for her gas, not touching the money in her bra. In her purse was a compact, a gold tube of lipstick, gum wrappers, aspirin, a few crumpled bills, and the checkbook.

A middle-aged woman with bleached hair looked at her blankly from the cash register.

"Do you have a water fountain?" B. asked the woman.

The woman did not acknowledge her question, just put down her magazine and went back behind a gray door and emerged with a paper cup of water.

"You on your way to Reno?" the woman asked.

"No."

The woman looked annoyed.

"Do you sell maps?" B. asked.

The woman flicked her chin toward the back of the store. B. walked to a revolving rack. She picked up a map of the state. "Do you have anything just for the valley?" she called to the woman.

"The 'valley'?" The woman frowned. "That's all we have over there."

By the time B. returned to the counter the annoyance had set into the woman's features and she pushed the change toward B. and went back to her magazine without looking up again.

B. laid the map across the passenger seat. Hundreds of black names on pastel. She'd only wanted a small patch to concentrate on, just a piece. She folded the map up. The heat in the car and the smells of hot metal and plastic drugged her. She closed her eyes and leaned her head back against the square seat.

She must have fallen asleep because next the woman from the gas station was rapping at her windshield. "There's no loitering here," she said. "Can't just park all day at the pumps. We got other customers, you know."

B. rubbed her eyes. The woman glared at her. B. looked around; there were no other cars. "I'm sorry. I guess I was tired."

The woman crossed her arms, the tanned skin draping.

"Is there a bank somewhere around?" B. asked.

"Go back to Suisun City or on to Rio Vista. There's nothin' in between."

For a moment B. thought the woman said something else under her breath. But the woman only continued to glare from behind the sagging arms and B. had no way of knowing if she was right.

When she came on Suisun City, the small main street and the pale tiled buildings were quaint but the marina behind the town startled B. Just like that, a row of boats in blue-brown water, masts bobbing against the flat yellow. She felt suddenly that the bay was following her, leaking out in a last menacing grab through the marsh stalks.

She jotted a random amount on the check.

"Good afternoon, ma'am." The pretty teller standing among the calm straight lines and muted oil paintings.

"It's 'miss' actually."

"Oh, I'm sorry, ma'am. I mean, miss."

But the cool expansive feeling still came. B. felt so light and cheerful afterward, she considered shaking the girl's hand, then thought better of it. As she walked back to the Mustang, the odd, misplaced marina did not disturb her in the least.

BACK ON THE ROAD THE heat and sleepiness were too much. She searched for a motel and had to return to the freeway to find a motor inn with a billboard of a bikini-clad woman diving into a pool. B. did not turn on the air conditioner when she got inside the room, just let the heat melt over her as she lay on the bed.

She took the money out of her bra strap. It was now at least a dozen fifty-dollar bills; she had no interest in counting them. She rifled through the vinyl travel bag, pulling out for a moment the velvet box with the diamond brooch, then replacing it. Instead she took out a bottle of nail polish.

The room was darkening but she left off the light. She thought of nothing but smoothing the pale iridescent pink from the brush, of the nicely piquant smell. She'd watched her mother at her vanity making her *toilette*, the French word she'd taught B. for pinning her hair, applying her lipstick, dabbing a crystal perfume bottle at her neck. Each gesture accruing to her some invisible potency. Her mother had once given her the last tortoiseshell compact of her favorite face powder, a discontinued line, and B. kept it intact and untouched like a totem, unsure what might happen if she finished it.

When her nails were painted, B. lay down again with her palms flat against the bed and fell asleep.

She woke on her side, the nail polish fretted with lines from the bedspread. She had dreamed of the landscape from the car, the contourless vista, a stream of yellow and white and green with no signs of people, and in the dream she had decided she would follow this land forever.

2.

THE NEXT MORNING THE BLOOD of her period had soaked through the toilet paper in her underwear. There was only the slightest brush of it on the inside of her dress. She hesitated to change. It was as if quitting the dress would disturb a key element to her new, fluid state. To bathe she sponged her armpits and her crotch and inserted a new tampon and put on new underwear. She threw the stockings from the day before in the trash, feeling vaguely guilty, but it was too hot. Then she worked on her face, the moisturizer and powder, the liquid liner at her eyes and the lipstick and perfume last. She pinned her hair back in place. There were young girls in the city now who let their hair go naturally, who never wore makeup, whose clothes were ill-fitting. These girls distressed B.

She'd forgotten a toothbrush. She walked from the motel

toward a gas station. There was no town, only the motel (the pool in the daylight was small and chipped), a telephone booth, the gas station with a general store attached, and another street across the intersection. Her heels crunched in the pebbles along the road, the freeway cars moaning and thumping beside her. The morning sun already burned her shoulders. A watery-brown haze at the edge of the sky stung her eyes.

At the store, she bought a toothbrush and toothpaste, a doughnut and a cup of coffee.

"I'm just taking a tour of the valley," she found herself saying to the paunchy older man at the cash register. "I just thought it would be very interesting." She tried not to hear her own voice.

"Pretty hot time of year to choose." The man's neck was a loose pink.

"Well, I don't have anything pressing in town right now. Nothing I can't miss."

The man nodded as if this was clear and handed her the doughnut and paper cup.

As she drank the coffee in the shade of the building outside, she told herself there would be no police after her. What she'd done was not big or serious enough. And she was pretty. People had always seemed to like this. Her nose was aquiline, her lids heavy but eyes almond-shaped, this combination giving her, she'd been told, a bedroom quality. She had never experienced this quality but understood it appealed to people and so drew her eyeliner out to feline points at the sides of her eyes and kept her hair blonde. She was aware from the ballet lessons her mother had required that she moved with her shoulders down and neck long, which people also took to be ladylike and contented.

She walked across the intersection to the other street in the non-town. Two houses stood on it, one boarded up. The other was hidden by a wooden fence that when she peered inside was overrun with cacti. The cacti had clawed over a single arch of walkway to the door; everything else in the bramble dead and dry. A walnut tree bowed over the porch. The smell of dog feces baked in the sun, although no dog to be seen.

She opened the gate. (There were things she would not have done in the city: she'd wanted to enter a yard on one of the hills and peer into the mudroom at children's windbreakers on hooks and dirty sneakers lined up; she'd stopped herself.) She stooped under the cacti. The freeway blew; no dog barked. When she reached the door, she knocked without a clear reason. She had a sense the owner here lived alone, and she wanted to speak with him. She could tell the person she was new to the valley, ask for tips. The windows were layered in dust. She knocked again louder. On the porch under the windows was a collection: an enameled pot, several stones, tines of sharp antlers. B. glanced around. She slipped a small antler bone into her purse. For luck.

In the car, on the freeway, the non-town was already behind her. She tried to think of some current pop song, something fresh and summery to sing, but in truth she did not like the songs on the radio now. So she hummed her favorite parts from *The King and I.*

It was 1967. In the spring she had turned thirty.

3.

B. HAD ONCE WATCHED A boy playing in a sandbox in the city. In a playground in her neighborhood, perched like all the playgrounds in the city, it seemed to her, precariously on a hill, as if it might fall off the side of the world. The mothers had been pretty in their makeup and scarves, their clipped, determined movements—hands darting in and out of a pram, through a small child's hair with leaves—admirable to B. But it was too draining to watch the women; they spoke too vehemently about items and opinions she did not understand. Her attention had settled instead on the boy. He poured the sand over his hand with such concentration, such absorption at the run of the dry grains on his fingers, that nothing else mattered, nothing else touched him. Only the feel of the sand on his skin and the keeping of its cascading rhythm. B. watched the boy until the mothers called him away, and after they'd gone she felt strangely abandoned, as if she should have spoken to him. She got up and looked around to make sure no one was watching and then sat in the sandbox. Following the boy's movements, she poured the sand over her hand, but she felt only the irritating papery sensation on her skin and when her knees began to ache from kneeling, she got up and left.

She decided that the checks were for her like the sand for the boy, and she did not let her mind go beyond this thought.

4.

THE RADIO ANNOUNCED A HEAT wave for the valley. B. could not imagine it any hotter. The back of the ivory sheath had sweat through and her limbs felt swollen; her hair had half slipped out of its pins. She stopped at a restaurant on an exit. She brought her large makeup case into the bathroom and powdered and fixed her hair and unzipped her dress to spray perfume underneath.

She ordered an iced tea from the waiter. The young man stared at her so intensely she wondered for a moment if she knew him from somewhere. She asked if he lived nearby, and he nodded without speaking. She remarked on the heat and he continued to stare until finally he said, "Ma'am, your zipper's undone."

She reached her hand to her back; her dress was flared open. "Oh. Thank you." She flushed to her neck. Her bra strap had fallen down her shoulder and she smelled her own odor still pungent under the perfume. She gripped the zipper awkwardly and pulled it up as far as she could. "Thank you," she mumbled. After he left, she pretended to study the menu with great absorption.

A woman with three small children was the only other customer in the place. She sat two tables over but kept staring at B. and the sky-blue makeup case. The woman looked old and childlike at the same time, small-boned, a high forehead with deep lines. She was wearing a sundress with a stain at the breast. In one arm she held a baby, while two young children ran back and forth from the window to the table, eating half a French fry and dropping it on the floor, sucking the juice off a pickle and putting it back. The woman sat like a statue in the midst of it.

"Do you live around here?" B. asked.

The woman's expression signaled the ridiculousness of the question. The baby squirmed. She hitched it higher and tighter on her lap without once glancing at it.

"I was just wondering if there was anything of interest to visit. For someone passing through."

The woman looked at B. as if she had asked for directions to China. A strand of thin hair fell across the lined forehead.

"There's Old Town, I guess," the woman said finally. "If you like the gold rush stuff. They have a railroad museum there, I think." One of the children ran by and shoved the baby. The baby smiled wildly as if it was a game and not an aggression.

"Oh, I won't be going to Sacramento, actually."

The woman seemed to accept this as understandable. "There's the buttes," she went on. "On the way to Chico. Those are sort of strange. Just strange to look at, out there all alone. But they don't let you drive in them. It's private land, I guess." She paused. "There's not much to see before Tahoe really."

"They sound lovely. Thank you."

B. absently fingered the handle of the makeup case.

"I'm from the city," B. added.

The mother nodded curtly as if to put a stop to this need to state the obvious. The baby was kicking its legs and whining. It tried again to scootch off her lap but the woman's grip seemed an insensate vice. The baby gave up and sank back into watching the children, trapped, mesmerized.

"You travelin' alone?" the woman asked.

"Yes."

"You lost or something?"

"No. Just driving. Just taking in the sights."

The mother picked up a French fry and swirled it in ketchup without eating it. "Well, I'd go directly on to Reno if I was you. There's nothing to see before Reno. A lot of driving gets me irritated."

The baby finally let out its wail then, sharp and steady. The mother hauled it to her shoulder and slapped it on the cheek, which only made the baby cry louder. Just then an adolescent boy opened the door of the restaurant and yelled, "We're parked in the back, he's waiting, come on!" The woman scooped up her purse and the baby and barked at the children to follow.

"Well, good luck with your trip," she said over the baby's shrieks. "The buttes, I guess, but I don't know if they're worth it." And in a burst of chaos and sun, she was gone.

The waiter finally brought her iced tea and B. twirled the straw, letting the ice circle. She looked out the window at the Mustang in the parking lot. The blue metallic sheen was already filmed with dirt. She tried to imagine the buttes. In her mind they were snub-nosed, western, angular, removed. She left her tea and went back to the bathroom. Her eyeliner was still intact but her pores large again and her lipstick gone. She reapplied the powder and twisted up the lipstick and told herself once more that she was just taking in the sights, making an anthropological tour of the valley. A survey, she considered vaguely in the mirror. She drew on the pale pink until her lips were bloodless.

5.

"IT'S NOTHING YOU HAVE TO worry about. It's nothing that touches you. I just want it off my chest. I don't want to bring that shit into this."

That was how the checks began: Daughtry had used them on a trip to Carmel. He'd driven her down the coast to a restaurant with white tablecloths and a view of the ocean, where the chicken was mealy and the carrots oversweet and elevator music piped out through invisible speakers. He had insisted she taste his abalone although she nearly gagged and could not reconcile the notion that the runny meat had nestled inside the jeweled interiors of shell. He ordered champagne and blathered on about the drive.

"Those mansions on all those cliffs, dammit! Those rich people knew exactly where we would want to sightsee and now we get their walls and garages. 'Scenic drive' bullshit. Fucking criminals. Imagine taking your whiskey there every night, the ocean and those crazy pine trees and just watching the sun set . . . You wouldn't have a care in the world. Who would?"

His nervous chatter was what helped her. About a lousy base-ball pitcher or the shape of her face or the city degraded by the "hippie trash." So she did not have to think or deflect anything from her mind while he spoke. She could concentrate on his deeply felt conviction in each phrase, wrap her mind around the banal images and observations, and before she knew it an hour had passed. And when his head canted and the hangdog, self-defeating look came over him at some gaffe he'd made—an expletive, an ignorance of some kind—she might even reach out and stroke his cheek.

But on the way out of the city that day Daughtry had been unusually quiet. His palm damp as he cupped her shoulder, the car door not closed all the way when he ran into the bank, so it blew rhythmically as cars barreled by on California Street.

"What's wrong?" she'd asked. But he did not speak until they got past Daly City and then he only talked about getting out of the "rat-race city."

It was not until after the white-tableclothed restaurant, when they had gone back to a motel on the main drag in Carmel, that Daughtry, drunk, had confessed about the checks.

"I don't want you to get the wrong impression, it's not that I want to do these things, but it's always the money thing, you know. Who isn't behind the eight ball every once in a while? You can get canned pretty easily when you're not union, and the union scene with the dues and the fucking meetings . . . It's just been a way to tide over. You, you don't have to worry about stuff like that. You make their offices look good."

She'd met Daughtry in the building where she worked. He came to their floor to fix dead lightbulbs, unclog toilets. (She once saw him huddled against a window because one of the girls lost her earring behind a heating vent.) His smile was large, his voice raspy. He was not very tall. His hair was black and thick and combed with oil and he had light green eyes. "I like your hair up that way," he told her one day as she ate a sandwich at her desk and read her book. He had on his coveralls and was carrying a hammer; she did not know his first name. "Most men want it down all the time," he said, "but it gives you class." Her hair was thick and in between the wash-and-sets she pinned it up in a French twist. She thanked him and burrowed into her page, trying to ignore him as he stood there.

"You don't look like a secretary," he went on.

"I am a secretary," she answered.

"But I see you read all those books."

"That doesn't mean I'm not a secretary," she said, and she got up and excused herself to the bathroom.

He was undeterred. The next day he found her outside on the concrete steps in the brief sun that passed between the wisps of fog, her arms goose-pimpled in her cardigan, and he told her she was too good for that office. She had gone to college, he could tell just by looking at her, been raised in a good family. She told him then she wished he would leave her alone. He nodded as if he'd known she would say it. And he did leave her alone after that, a look of melancholy on his face any time their eyes met.

But on her bus ride in the evenings through Chinatown, looking out on the mashed vegetables on the sidewalk and the Chinese rushing for home with their paper bags, only to leave new rotting vegetables on the sidewalk the next day, she thought of Daughtry. Or she remembered her musty dark apartment waiting for her, and she thought, I'll have a drink with him. Why not? And he told her he would take her away from the city.

So they had gone to Carmel.

In the motel room, sitting on the bed, the hard grooves of his black hair coming undone, still in his leather blazer, Daughtry had cried. "You're fancy. I wanted to do something fancy for you. But I can't get back into the checks. I did it this one time, there's no way they can peg the one on me. But I'm never going back to jail again." He got up and vomited in the toilet and returned to the bed and now his hair was mopped forward, his nose red and his green eyes sallow. He stretched out on the comforter and began to tell her, although she had not asked, how it was done. She lay next to him, listening as he explained each step of the crime. "You don't want just any account numbers, you want it from the right mailboxes, in the right zip codes . . . It's like you and the teller are in this dance, and she takes a step and you take a step and as long as you don't step on her toes, you're free."

And she realized as he spoke that the carsickness had gone away. The nausea or ringing or tightness or whatever it was that was back now worse than in the East, had momentarily disappeared. When Daughtry switched to his childhood in the Irish neighborhood with the cramped stucco houses—on and on, about the freeway cutting it up and his drunk mother—she asked him to go back to the checks.

"You like the bad-boy stuff, huh? You like to slum?" She just wanted to understand, she said. "Well, alright, baby. I do happen to have a certain style for these things . . ."

She'd listened intently to this man—to whom she was not in truth attracted, whose breath reeked of liquor and vomit, with whom she would spend the night—tell her about money he had stolen to take her to a forgettable dinner in Carmel. And she had felt better.

6.

She had been in San Francisco two years. It was not the weather that had drawn her; she liked the fall leaves and the snow and the humid nights in the East well enough. It was not, as it seemed for the young people who came that spring, with their grass-smoking and greasy hair, the idea of a counterculture, the attraction of some newer, freer community opposing itself to the mainstream; she had no objection to the mainstream. She could not say the exact reason she had come west except that she thought it would help.

What needed helping was hard to pin down. She only knew that it had to do with the carsickness. She could not take walks anymore and she could not be with people, she could not go to the movies or have a drink or visit a museum or read a book without feeling carsick. This was her only term for it. It

simulated the thin buzzing nausea of sitting in the backseat of
an ever-curving car, except it was not at all related to motion.
"Nausea" was not the term either, too clinical and specific. It
was not a migraine or a flu. It was the slightest spinning sensation gripping the back of her neck. Like a slow, pitched whine
at the outer edge of her skull, behind her eyes, in the joints of
her jaw. It was almost imperceptible at first, as if a small humming switch had been left on in her head. But it always grew. It
was worst on weekends. The long stretches of free time without
occupation—she was relieved to work, to type letters and stuff
envelopes at her office jobs, although she did not enjoy it, was
not stimulated by it—ineluctable days, no matter sunny or dark,
like a dull disc hanging over her, giving off a relentless cardboard
light. On the weekends, she tried to divide the days into tenable
units. Mornings, to sit with coffee and the newspaper until at
least ten o'clock, even if her body buzzed, if her vision blurred
with tension. She did not allow herself to clench anything, to go
back to bed. If she could make it through newspaper and coffee,
she could next turn to some cleaning or tidying task, necessary
or not—pulling out every scarf from her dresser and refolding
them, for example—until a decent enough time to turn to pre-
paring lunch. Here she made her movements agonizingly slow,
scooping out one flaky chunk of tuna at a time, layering in a
single spoonful of mayonnaise, dropping single bits of celery
and onion, and then repeating the whole exercise over again.
When her lunch was ready, she waited with her plate at the

table until exactly noon, no sooner. After lunch, anything to keep busy, the walks, a museum if she could bear it—reading never worked at its worst—any activity to stretch the time until mid-afternoon, late afternoon on good days. At that point she could return to her apartment and take a nap or sit by her window watching the light dim. Only then could she reassure herself of the sloping of the day toward evening. Darkness the goal. Darkness to kill the day.

As though forgetting that weekends would still exist there, she had chosen to believe as others in the restorative powers and newness of the West for her own purposes. That a change to the West might help.

And for a while, the new city did help. For the first year, the beauty had awed and distracted her (Boston had been a hill city, too, but the hills were small and heavy and rust-colored in her mind) and she'd been buoyed like everyone else by the pale and white buildings, the fuchsia bougainvillea, the sails on the water and whiffs of orange blossom and jasmine in winter. She'd ridden the cable car to work and eaten crab sandwiches at the wharf, listened to street music in the Italian neighborhood. She had liked to take walks, to spots known for some reputed charm—a robin's-egg-blue Victorian; a brooding WPA mural; a grove of redwoods in the middle of the park. Once or twice, perhaps, the sight of a young unkempt man with a guitar, the smell of body oil they wore or the absence of handbag and stockings had disturbed the calming effect, had brought on the small buzzing at the back of her skull. But it had not lasted very long.

The first thing to give way had been the buses. She had been accustomed to subways and elevateds in the East, but the main mode of travel around the city was the buses, and on them she could not read a book or write a letter because it made her dizzy, and so she was forced to spend the time looking and thinking. Every morning through Chinatown the painfully thin men wearing second-hand baseball caps for teams they did not follow and the women with their hair cut mannishly short, beautiful cheek bones with missing teeth, and the mounds of vegetables to be bought, and the stands to be dragged into place and filled and haggled over and emptied, and everything to start over the next day. She did not understand why it brought back memories like the prom with the Brylcreemed boy: sitting around with Cokes in her peach-colored satin dress and the gardenias on her wrist and the diamond brooch on her bust. The Brylcreemed boy telling her she was pretty and leading her around the floor and asking her to wear his pin at the next prom. Something in this memory felt like the Chinese and their vegetables. But how could this be anything like the Chinese and their vegetables? She couldn't puzzle it out. So she tried to observe a sliver of the bay, with its whitecaps and sailboats, or a majestic bridge, or the exotic red calligraphy in the shop windows; but none of it helped. And so she came to hate the buses.

Then she had been unable to find a beauty parlor she liked.

It disturbed her acutely, the young women in the city walking around with long stringy hair and faces bare. This increased B.'s zeal to find the right salon, as if she were taking a stand against those other girls. She visited a half dozen salons in different neighborhoods, always finding some fault, in how her curls were set, in the too kitschy or too plain décor. In fact there was nothing manifestly wrong with these places: what she sought she could not have described in plain concrete terms, even to herself. She'd come close once or twice. In a salon in the nicest hill neighborhood, the walls had not been too pink or gold, the seats filled with women who seemed not too old or all married. She'd struck up a conversation with a woman at the dryers.

"Whatever happened to a little smoothing out? A little help?" the woman said, pointing to a bra advertisement in a magazine without accompanying girdle. B. had smiled.

"You remember that movie where Liz Taylor was insane, in the convent?" The woman's nails were blood red.

"The Tennessee Williams play."

"Right! And then Monty Clift let her have her hair done and 'wear a pretty dress' in the state bin, and presto, she's still loony but at least now she has a waist!"

B. smiled again, but a genuine smile that she might have in private. "And he falls in love," she said.

"You see? Right there, that's the power of foundation garments!"

But then something in the conversation spoiled. The woman

began complaining about a man she was dating ("He's next to a telephone *all day*. There's nothing to prevent him from *picking it up* and *dialing*.") and her voice sounded to B. like a high-pitched cry in an animal register. The spinning and nausea came on abruptly. After that, B. stopped trying to find a favorite beauty parlor and got her wash-and-sets wherever it was cheapest.

Finally, there had been the bridge. It was a cliché, she knew, her love for it, but she had been drawn by the sheer size, its serious red color—not golden at all—and she went there almost every Sunday, standing in the middle of the span on the ocean side (the tourists preferring the bay side for the city views when the Pacific was the real wonder to her mind). The fog blew in like a divine force, the cables vibrating in the wind, and she saw the Spanish landing for the first time, and the sailors and priests and forty-niners, and she briefly forgot time and place, until her teeth chattered and the ocean was lost in fog.

When she'd heard the siren, she had not immediately absorbed what was going on. Only later did B. understand that a woman not far down from her had gone over the railing. No interruption in the gust of cars or the vibrations of the cables or the tourists' voices. A family of Germans who'd seen it told her the woman had been a teenager, that she'd worn plastic-frame glasses and a blue dress and tennis shoes. (B. could never absorb this last detail; she would always imagine the girl in kitten heels.) B. lingered near the Germans as they gave their eyewitness reports to the police, hoping the hearing of it would confer the realness of the incident on her. But the girl was just gone; she did not have any feeling about it. B. stood at the spot until the fog came in and finally made her depart. She did not visit the bridge again.

7.

"JOEY LOVES THE HAZELNUTS."

"Joey hates nuts."

"We'll get him the hazelnuts and Aunt Edie the walnuts."

Billboards for the theme park had been on every highway: a playground to promote the local nut crops, with restaurant and gift shop and its own choo-choo train. As if in capitulation, she'd stopped. Now she wandered around the rocking horses and carousel, among the families on their way to Tahoe and Reno waiting for cocktails and burgers in the lounge or picnicking outside. She felt conspicuous, as if the already-wrinkled ivory sheath announced to them that she was on her way to neither the mountains nor the lake, that she had not packed for a vacation per se. She watched the families eat their peanut butter and jellies and drink their thermosed lemonade and tried to imagine herself as one of the mothers. Cajoling the children, scrubbing their dwarfed hands, dusting off their bottoms. But she couldn't keep herself inside the smells, the textures, the gummy breath, the tiny eyelashes. She went into the gift shop.

"He loves nuts, I tell you, he lives for them," the wife said. She and the husband both in loud prints. "He eats about a pound if I put them out before supper."

"That's not the Joey I know," the husband said. "The Joey I know never ate a nut in his life."

"We'll get him the almonds then."

She wondered what Joey really wanted. Did he want almonds or hazlenuts, or no nuts at all? Something about this line of thought and the rows of tightly wrapped cellophane packages done up in bows made the spinning come on quickly. She bought a bag of pecans and hurried out.

She ran back to the Mustang, thinking she must find the antler bone. To rub it or sit with it, so it might calm her. But when she sat in the hot air with the bone in her lap, the carsickness only increased. She turned the ignition and screeched out of the nut-theme parking lot toward the nut town's main street and bank as if there wasn't a moment to lose.

Her trembling slanted the writing on the check.

"I feel much better," she said out loud.

The teller looked at her as if she understood. "That's wonderful, ma'am. Enjoy your trip to Reno."

Afterward, she pored over every detail: the chilled air on her flushed skin, the right angles of the teller windows, the teller's movements like a soothing port de bras. The girl's face, young and full, her two front teeth indented winsomely, a white Peter Pan collar and nude nail polish. And the shade of ivory on the walls that B. swore she had not seen in years, that had given way to the mustard yellows and lime greens exclusively, although she could not prove it.

She pored over these details because it was never the money she did it for.

8.

"I DON'T SEE WHY IT'S so difficult for you," her mother had said. She'd called to tell B. she was sending an embroidery kit. So that B. would know how to embroider for any occasion. "There's an order to things," she told B., "and I think it would help if you followed it."

"I'd like to." B. nodded into the receiver.

"You can, dear. Just try a little harder."

"I will."

But in the end B. could not bring herself to ask where this order began or how she had missed it or why it seemed to her mother so easy a thing to pick up.

9.

She drove on a two-lane road. The sun bore down on the car. For miles, nothing but the sere, parchment-colored fields, populated sporadically by black cows and rectangular stacks of yellow hay (it must be hay, she thought; it would be more solid, she would be better situated, she felt, if she could know these things for certain). The only vertical structure a line of skeletal electrical towers. She passed an outdated sign advertising July Fourth fireworks at the river. Then below it in red letters: CAUTION: GRASS FIRE RISK EXTREME.

Eventually the road rounded and a few trees appeared. Houses, signs to the delta. She would hit the river soon, and if she continued too far along it, she would come to the capital. She took note of this.

The road came through a small town with a few businesses,

an auto mechanic, a burger stand, boat rentals, and as soon as she was through it the road curved and she was alongside the river. She parked the Mustang on the shoulder of the levee road. The levee rose high up from the water, tall green stalks on one side, which might be corn, or else sugar cane (again she felt vexed, undermined, not to know for sure); on the other side of the river, dozens of rows of full pear trees. The river was low and brown, but still she thought how nice it would be to swim— it had been ages since she'd been swimming. She noticed an elderly man fishing down the bank and wished she were alone.

She hadn't been swimming since her last trip to the lake house. Throughout her childhood her family had spent summer weekends at a lakeside cottage, where she and her mother had swum—her father never coming up until late Saturday or not at all. (In a faraway foreign land of legal pads and Dictaphones was how B. imagined him.) She and her mother swam and sun-bathed and painted their nails, did their hair and read their books. And then one day after college her mother had informed her that she wasn't welcome back alone. "It's just not produc-tive to come on your own anymore, darling," her mother had said, her voice full of encouragement. "Even a group would be better, don't you think?"

B. had lost her favorite pair of gloves on that last visit. A light cotton pair, white with almost imperceptible red dots. On the bed, off her hands, they looked to her like those of a circus performer, the dwarfish child-women who rode horses standing up. But on her hands they were beautiful and delicate, a living porcelain. She'd brought them despite the heat and the trend away from gloves, for the occasional drive into town. But when she searched her suitcase they were gone. She'd hyperventilated slightly, she remembered, as if she'd misplaced her own hands.

She looked down at her hands pink and swollen in the reflection from the river. She'd liked wearing gloves when it was the fashion. She could spend forty-five minutes looking for a lost one and feel as though she had spent the time as a person she knew how to be. Without the gloves, she had to adjust herself to feeling the dirt on trolley straps directly on her skin, to seeing women's hands everywhere naked and raw. Her own hands with veins and hatches and mounds of epidermis. (And again her mind jumped at the young women in the city now who not only did not wear gloves, but did not wear heels or put on lipstick or comb their hair.) B. still kept her old gloves in a satin-covered box in her closet; she knew exactly how many pairs there were, which needed mending, which had stains; the kid gloves shriveled and waiting on top. She could not bring herself to throw them away.

She took off her heels and climbed down the riverbank to the stairs of a dock. She walked to the end and sat, dipping her feet in the water. The combination of the hot sun and the cold water was soothing and she let herself sit circling her shins lazily. The man down the bank had not moved. B. could not see his face, just the white hair under a hat and the drooped shoulders, and yet his presence agitated her, as if he could overhear her mind running.

She closed her eyes and tried in the heat and soothing water to daydream. She had difficulty daydreaming. There seemed a list of things she should be daydreaming about, what she knew the other secretaries daydreamed of: men, marriage, babies, money. But what came to her mind were never these things. What came to her mind were cool blue-white landscapes, featureless planes of snow or sand with no people or time. Whenever she made herself daydream about the secretaries' list, things like the developer and Sherry came up.

It was at a barbecue, one of the secretaries had invited B. during her first season in the city, also in the nicest hill neighborhood. She would have gone to the park with a book, but she knew her mother would ask later in their weekly phone call whether B. had "mingled" over the weekend. It was a rare hot and fogless day when one could go into the evening without a sweater, which made the city feel like a white-washed Mediterranean *ville* and made B. hopeful that something unexpected, even unrecognizable, might happen. When she walked into the party, all the women looked to be the same age (mid-twenties), most blonde like B., nails manicured and hair set, orange and pink and yellow dresses; the men wore button-down shirts and Bermudas and looked ill at ease and shiny in the heat.

One of the men approached B. right away, two vodka tonics in his hand, a sheen of sweat on his neck. "Thought I'd say hullo," he said, handing her one of the drinks. "Official unofficial welcoming committee." On first glance his face was handsome, smooth and symmetrical with gray placid eyes and clear skin. But as he spoke, B. noticed that his eyebrows were too thin or too faint, so that he resembled one of the anemic subjects of a medieval Dutch painting. He worked in real estate.

"It's a boom time for us, you know, it's all happening down 101—cineplexes, mini-malls. I'm Sherry's." He pointed to a woman across the deck who looked, except for her red hair, exactly like B. in her short bright sheath and matching headband. "We're just engaged."

The back deck of the house was small and crowded and B. felt beads of sweat in the boning of her bra. As he went on, there seemed to her something disturbingly missing, some void of detection in the Dutch eyebrowless face, as if he were talking not to her but to her teeth.

"Really, it's simple, you work a couple of years and then you get out of the race, down the peninsula. The weather is perfect, fog always lifts. Have you been? I could drive you down." He seemed unaware or unconcerned that he'd already told her about his fiancée. B. thought for a moment he might be drunk, but he seemed oddly sober, only growing too exuberant, almost jumpy, a twitch under his eye. "You really ought to see it. You'd like it better down there. Easy little yards and roads you can actually drive and mile-long grocery stores." He leaned toward her and his perspiration smelled sour. "Don't get me wrong, the city's hip, the city's *stimulating*, but it's no place to raise children. The other day we were tossing around a few balls at the park—do you play? Sher and I lost one of our doubles—and these head-shaved loonies in their dresses lined the court, chanting that Oriental hokum. I thought to myself, let the freaks have the city, I'll take Shangri-La."

When he tried unsuccessfully a few minutes later to kiss B., Sherry was suddenly at his side, locked into his arm as though nothing had happened. Without missing a beat, the developer explained how he and Sherry had met—"Goddamn right 'golden state' when the prettiest woman at the broker's office is a good Lutheran from Ohio with straight-ahead morals and a great pair of legs!" To this Sherry nodded, red hair perfectly curled, her arm clenched around the developer's like a vice. B. realized then with an abrupt but diffuse kind of terror that it wasn't just their outfits that were similar, it was the way the developer looked at them. With the same missing part of his gaze. A shudder went through her and she dropped her highball. Sherry stooped to the shards and the developer went for a broom, and B. excused herself and slipped out of the party.

She could try to daydream about Daughtry. She felt the carsickness slightly less with him, with his endless chattering, his graceless ways. Her initial, un-thought-out belief was that he could take her away somehow. She didn't know what she meant by *away* any more than she'd known what she meant by *help*. But the workingman calluses on Daughtry's hands, their roughness when he guided her by the back of her neck into his coupe, made her feel he existed in a real, visceral way the anemic-looking developers could not. And so she had tried to overlook their differences, to convince herself they were an asset. For the Carmel trip, she'd bought a merry widow—an optimistic, pale pink lace in the corseted body, rosettes at the top of its garters. She'd bought a new dress and matching heels at I. Magnin. On the way home from Carmel Daughtry said, "We had a good time, didn't we, baby? We saw the ocean, right? And I'll get you to like abalone one day. I'll get you to like me." Then he laughed too loudly, his face tensed. He was a good person underneath the slicked hair and the gauche talk, B. thought. Probably better than she.

She watched a beer can float by on the river. A faintly sulfurous scent wafted up from the water. She got up and made her way back to the car.

Hungry, she drove back to the town with the burger stand. It was a small shack, rusted-metal outdoor seats and a window counter. A collarless cat bolted around the corner as B. approached. Through the window she ordered a cheeseburger and a Coke from a thin teenage boy. She did not have enough money in her purse, so she excused herself to the dingy bathroom around back and took one of the fifties from her bra strap. But when she returned the teenage boy stared at the bill on the counter. "We don't have enough change for that, ma'am." The boy and B. both flushed. She slipped the stolen bill back into her purse. When she turned to leave, the teenager called her back and said under his breath he'd put it on the house.

There was a group of men sitting a few seats down. They were not much older than she, perhaps in their mid-thirties, with cloudy forearm tattoos, angular and leathered skin from too much sun. They talked and laughed tersely. B. sat down at one of the outdoor tables and picked up a left-behind news-paper to appear occupied. She flipped to a picture of the first lady and the president. B. had always preferred Lady Bird to Jackie, who was too aloof and enigmatic. Lady Bird with her dull matching suits and hair correctly curled would understand B.'s growing concern about the young women with unstyled hair. She would be equally dismayed at the unmatched clothes, the sitting in parks and dancing to guitars and smoking marijuana, the absence of stockings. And Lady Bird, she knew, would be most disturbed by the hazy blitheness in their eyes, as if beati-tude came from disarray, as if one could go through life with nothing else expected of them.

B. sensed the men watching her in between their laconic exchanges.

Yes, she felt someone like Lady Bird ought to take the situ-ation of the unstockinged young women in hand. As a national epidemic, a degenerative trend.

B. was gazing on the photo, lost in these thoughts, when one of the men was suddenly next to her.

"You lost, miss?"

"No." She searched the pick-up window for her cheese-burger. The window was shut, the teenager gone.

She saw the man glance at her ring finger. "That your car?" He flicked his chin at the Mustang. He had seen her park it.

"Looks new," he said.

"It is."

"Give you a good run, I bet."

"Yes."

Her cheeseburger came up then. She excused herself to the counter and thanked the boy again, who blushed and mumbled something back. He had forgotten the Coke; she could not bring herself to ask for it. She pretended to start eating and the man went back to his friends, his smell of gasoline and sweat lingering. She ate a part of the bun and a few bites of meat but lost her appetite and folded the wrapper. The man came back.

"You travelin' alone?" A look of amusement crossed his broad face. He leaned against the counter and looked directly at her.

She noticed the narrowness of his hips in his leather belt. She wondered if the narrowness made him feel light, easy to move. She did not want to look him in the eye. "Yes, I am."

"Well, I can give you directions if you like."

"I don't need any directions, thank you."

The deep lines at his mouth made him seem as if he was smirking at all times. "Well, I just thought . . . Well, a pretty lady like you might need some assistance."

"No thank you."

The smirk remained. He tipped his cap. "Well then, safe travels."

She gathered her purse and walked past him back to her car, feeling his eyes on her. She fumbled for the keys and started the engine and as she was about to back out she saw the men watching her still. Without thinking, she killed the engine. She exited the car and walked up to the man.

"I know exactly where I'm going, actually. I don't need any directions."

She could hear sniggering. "You said that." The man tipped his cap again. "Didn't mean to offend, miss." She went back to the car and sat behind the wheel and stared at them. She stared, losing track of time, until they began kicking the ground self-consciously. Then she started the engine again and backed out of the parking lot.

BACK AT THE LEVEE ROAD, she crossed a metal drawbridge to the other side of the river, running beside hundreds of trees with endless ghostly pods (she drove into the orchard itself and decided they were almonds). She came on a town the length of two blocks, with brick façades and an old hotel. Then farther down the levee beyond hunched old walnut trees, a dry feed store, a meat market, an old stone church.

And a bank.

She brought her focus back to the river. It was low, barely grazing the middle of the levees, still and brown as earth.

She followed the walnut trees along the road until she got too close to the capital, then veered away from the river and back out into the fields.

10.

"How do you act?" she'd asked him. "When you do it?"

"Look," he said, "the truth is, shopkeepers, tellers—chicks especially, I hate to tell you, baby—they ain't expecting them to be fake. They're thinking about the transaction, about getting their cut or doing their job, and fake money looks like real money, and fake checks look like real checks, so why would they think any different? Why would they suspect anything unless you gave them a reason to?" As he spoke an excitement and urgency grew in his voice, as if he were teaching a young boy the fundamentals of a ball game. "You gotta remember: you're the one who'll give it away, not the paper. I don't go in when I'm nervous. Only when I'm feeling cool. Today, normally, I would have junked it. But you were waiting in the car and I had the trip planned and that was that. You're shaky, you're sweating, you look funny, you don't do it. This should be the most obvious thing, but people are stupid."

"What if they stop you?" B. asked.

"You know how many steps it is to an exit. There were eighteen steps today. Twelve if I ran. I don't walk in without knowing how many it takes to get out. And usually I got heat."

The mention of the gun did not faze her. "Does it make you feel better?"

"What d'you mean?"

"Just in general, do you like the way it makes you feel?" She felt adrenaline rising in her chest.

He paused to consider. "Maybe. Maybe it's like you feel a little smarter than you did before. Like now you're the boss. But it isn't like I do it for kicks, if that's what you mean. Anyone who does it for kicks is a fool."

"Not for kicks, no," she agreed.

His eyes were full of her. He pulled her in. "Let's forget about that dirty stuff. I don't think I've said a proper hello. Gotta give a pretty lady her due." He put his fingers in her mouth to suck, and she knew she could not ask any more about the checks.

THE MORNING SHE HAD CALLED Daughtry about the checks, she'd seen a blue crocus during a walk. (She had not known what else to do but keep up the walks in the nice hill neighborhoods.) The blue of the flower with purple tones as if risen out of an underground pool, the miniature cups like perfect pagoda towers. Proof of the beauty of living and the grace of a higher hand, of hope unfolding. And yet it did not enter her. No part of the crocus came inside her, touched her in any way. Her head spinning on and on as if she would die. And she had thought suddenly, inexplicably, of the checks. She'd thought: the walks had not helped and the crocus had not helped but the checks would help.

And she had called Daughtry.

11.

SHE DROVE NORTH ALONG A two-lane road. The hot wind through the car made her body thick and slow. She came on an unkempt field. Plants tumbled on the ground in no order; she thought at first they must be abandoned. But the disorderliness continued from one field to the next, on and on, and eventually B. realized it must have some point and the heaps were tomato plants. Vines not tied up but splayed on the ground, leaves and fruit chaotic shades of green, yellow, red. An isolate string of eucalyptus trees bordered one side of the field. In its shade was a piece of rusted farm machinery (a thresher? combine?) and B. had the sudden urge to climb it.

She parked the car, walked over to the high metal engine, trying to ascertain its function to no avail, then hoisted herself up onto the dirty seat. Her bare legs hung down thin and pale near the gears. For miles in any direction the jumbled green plants, the faded blue sky. She closed her eyes, and in the warm, eucalyptus-spiced air, the radio song came into her mind, from the prom with the Brylcreemed boy: *One lovely night, Some lovely night.* She could not remember the rest. In fact, she realized, the only vivid recollection she had of the evening was the violent itch from the wire in her bustier, clawing at herself the minute she got the dress off that night, until flakes of skin drifted from her breasts and red welts swelled on her torso and her fingernails filled with blood. She stopped trying to sing the song.

She tried instead to cheer herself with the dead buttons on the farm machinery. In the pleasurable clicks and tacks, she imagined herself in denim overalls, chewing on a stalk of wheat. She wished for an old red barn and a scarecrow but the tomato fields seemed to have no owners. In the dried grass under the eucalyptus bright orange poppies like flames stood. Hard as she tried, she could not find them beautiful. The wide petals and bare stems and sharp orange in the dead grasses jarred her.

Her eye caught the image of her naked shins on the gear shaft. Bumps of black stubble now sprouted across them. It felt lewd. In her office a new girl had arrived her entire first week without stockings, until the office manager forced her to put on a pair she kept in her desk. B. had been secretly relieved. The first protest she'd ever seen in Boston, people prostrate across railroad tracks to stop commerce to the South or Asia or some place, B. had fixated not on the cause or the chants but on the women's legs, the stockinged shins in pencil skirts and kitten heels. All the men in trousers and button-down shirts and sweaters, but the women's legs dainty across the gunmetal tracks, out of place like the poppies in the dead grass. B. had wondered how they'd lowered themselves without ripping their skirts or running their hose. (Her mother had taught her the proper manner to sit in a skirt: guide the fabric underneath, slide hands over the line of one's thighs, end with fingers folded neatly in lap; her mother had, aside from ski pants and the occasional summer capri, worn a dress every day of her life.) It had been naive, but B. had assumed in San Francisco people would be too sunned and relaxed to protest. Instead they protested all the time, in blue jeans and maxis and tunics and half naked, and B. could no longer hold on to anything in these scenes at all. She tried to avoid them.

Troubled by these thoughts, she climbed down from the rusty machine and kicked around in the fallen curved leaves of the eucalyptus, peeled off strips of blond bark. (The tomatoes she would not get too near.) She wondered how many checks she had in total; she'd never counted them. She got the checkbook out (she liked always to carry the ostrich-skin purse with her) and fanned it back and forth in her damp palms.

She decided she did not want to know how many there were.

A motorcycle thundered by at that moment, shattering the quiet. The motorcycles were all over the roads now, B. thought with disgust, the long pipes, the reclining riders in leather and suede.

She got in the car and drove back to one of the towns on the river. She found the old hotel, still fronted by rails for tying up horses. She lay on the poster bed until the whole room disappeared into dusk, the roses on the wallpaper turning black. Children's voices drifted through the window in the dimness, crickets bleating, somewhere a radio playing country-western. B. tried to focus on these sounds of domesticity and summer ease. She tried not to think about the bank three doors down.

She thought how much she loved the heat. In the fog and cold of the city, she had begun to forget the time of year. Was it June or December, she never knew.

12.

THAT NIGHT IN HER DREAM she was on the motorcycle. Dressed in black, fringe flying from her arms. The metal vibrating unstoppably between her legs. She began frantically in her sleep to feel for the edges of paper slips in boxes, to slide a check across a counter. She woke up, panting among the black roses. She reached for the antler, but rubbing it had no effect. To calm herself, she thought of what time the bank would open, which side she would part her hair, whether it would be the pink or the coral lipstick. She concentrated on each of these things until she was sure the motorcycle was gone.

13.

In the morning, she took a bath in the crumbling hotel tub. A ring of dirt rose to the surface. The black grit under her fingernails loosened and she washed her hair. When she emerged from the tub she picked up the ivory sheath from the hanger and reluctantly packed it back into her bag. She had laid out a fresh dress on the bed, a sleeveless powder blue. She combed through her wet hair and drew on eyeliner. Her period was still trickling in. She put in a tampon and washed the browned blood from her fingertips and reached into the vinyl bag for the velvet box.

Her parents had given her the diamond brooch when she turned sixteen. Her mother explained that the brooch marked her passage into womanhood; her great-grandmother had worn it at her wedding and her grandmother and her mother.

The brooch was in the shape of a daisy, twenty petaled chains of diamonds glinting from a dense center, so fragile and precise and dazzling it seemed it would transform her just to touch it. They'd brought out a cake with candles and after she blew them out, her mother pinned the diamond brooch on B.'s sweater, her father looking on embarrassedly. They took a picture of B. standing alone with the brooch in front of the cake.

She could recall wearing it to the prom with the Brylcreemed boy, and to her graduation luncheon and perhaps for a college mixer or two. One night in Boston, after the kind of typical day where she had shown up for work on time and done her typing and spoken politely to the attorneys and other secretaries and even had a date later that evening (one of a string of torturous set-ups through her mother during which she had the same conversation about Back Bay and the fall foliage each time), she took the velvet box out of the drawer. She pinned the brooch to her bra and stood in front of the full-length mirror. Her upper arms were muscular, her sternum hard with bone, and the brooch in the lamplight no longer looked precise and dazzling but sharp and overladen, like a brand, a deformity growing out of her. She yanked it off, the pin catching the bra and scraping her chest. Her head began to spin. She sterilized the cut, sewed up the bra and stuffed the velvet box, wrapped in several scarves, into the back of her closet. When the date arrived, she pretended to be sick.

B. stood in front of the motel mirror. The brooch shimmered against the powder-blue dress, but the effect was remote now. She fingered the encrusted petals and noticed her thumbnail was still dirty.

THE TWO WOMEN TELLERS EACH had long painted nails and teased hair, one blonde with softly flipped-up ends and the other brunette with a round, short style. They counted out the money to patrons, placing bills on the counter gently and politely as if setting out linens for tea.

"How far are the buttes from here?" B. heard herself asking the blonde teller.

"The buttes?" The young woman looked at her warmly, parentally, as if B. had spoken nonsense. She had hooded light blue eyes. "You mean Middle Mountain."

"I guess so. I don't know the name. Someone told me about them."

"They're not far, you take Twenty east toward Colusa. But I don't think you can walk in them or anything."

"I just wanted to see them."

The teller nodded and again smiled patiently.

B. watched the teller place the check in a drawer and draw out the cash. She counted it quickly, a flash between her pink fingernails, then counted again, dealing it out on the counter. B. noted the neat rhythm, the tidy semicircle of cash. A tendril of the teller's blonde hair fell forward. B. touched her own to make sure it was in place.

"Is there a beauty parlor around here?" B. asked. "Your hair is very pretty."

The young woman smiled, still patient-looking. "If you go upriver. Jeannie's. They have new dryers, not too hot." She looked at B. sheepishly. "I really like your dress, and your brooch is lovely."

"Thank you. I. Magnin for the dress." Now came the cool expansive feeling. B. let it spread out her back, all the way to her fingers.

"I've always wanted to shop in the city."

"You should take a special trip."

B. gathered her bills and put them carefully in her purse. "Thank you," she said, and walked toward the door.

"Oh, ma'am?" B. was almost outside.

She turned around. The cool expansive feeling had settled throughout her now and the young teller floated like a pale blonde aura over the marble counter.

"You forgot your receipt," the teller said.

B. took the piece of paper. "Thank you so much."

"Have a nice drive."

She walked out of the bank with five hundred dollars.

It was fine now, everything was light. Along the levee road were lines of short leafy green plants bordered by dried yellow tufts of grass. B. stopped at a fruit stand and bought a bag of blackberries. She ate handfuls as she drove, the juice on her lips and fingers (she tried not to stain the powder-blue dress). She had a song in her head from the hotel lobby, about following along on a carousel—the ornate lacquered horses going round in her mind—and she wished for the song to be only about that.

Suddenly she wanted ice cream. She could not remember the last time she'd wanted ice cream. The cool expansive feeling carried her forward. She drove to the next town and asked around at the grocery store for a parlor and when the woman at the cash register told her there was none, she bought a tub of vanilla ice cream with a fifty-dollar bill. "Is there a spoon I could use?" she asked. The woman was still counting out her change, which B. dropped into the paper bag with the ice cream. The woman frowned and shook her head. "No spoons."

B. sat in the Mustang with the tub in her lap and scooped the ice cream into her mouth with her fingers. She tasted the bubbles in the cream, the liquor of the vanilla. It seemed in just the past few minutes the river had become bluer, the trees edged in gold. A man walked by the car in jean overalls, dirtied from some work in a field (or a barn?), whistling a tune. It sounded hopeful and familiar. Now, eating her ice cream, thinking of the driving and fields and endless road, she was buoyed. She sang the song from the long-ago prom again putting the wounding bustier out of her mind. Her singing voice was high and weak, but more of the words came back to her this time, and she was pleased that she'd put them together, as if she had locked onto something real.

When she'd had enough she left the ice cream tub on the car floorboard and climbed down the riverbank. She washed her hands and mouth and a blue jay screeched from a walnut tree. In the sun, near the water, her mind began to soar. She imagined a small house, herself in it, with light pouring through the windows, quiet all around. She walked along the riverbank and stumbled on more of the poppies. This time she picked a handful and studied them, as if to persuade herself of the beauty of the bright flaming orange. They had no scent. She brought the bouquet back to the car and laid it on the gear shaft, next to the antler bone. She would put them in a glass of water some-where. Maybe in a small house, a glass of water for her poppies.

A young Mexican wearing a stained white hip apron came out from behind a building and dumped a bag of trash. B. beamed at him. She smoothed her dress and sat at the wheel; her hands and face dried in the heat. She touched her fingers again to her hair, wondering how mussed it looked, and started the engine.

FOR A WHILE SHE PASSED through asparagus fields along the river. They looked at first like ferns but soon she noted the veg-etable stalks underneath, and her body hummed with a kind of power to recognize a crop by herself (before the hand-painted

sign advertising asparagus bunches). The ice cream and this recognition and the still-lightness from the bank kept her moving
along. Then she came to the sunflowers.

The stalks were mostly green but the flowers above were
dead and hanging. The bent brown heads and leaning stalks
made them look like a mass of defeated people, bound to go
forward. Slowing down for the sunflowers B. saw the chapel
standing in the middle of them.

She parked.

When she got near the sunflowers, they made a baleful dry
rattling sound, as if they were trying to talk to her. She tried not
to hear this.

B. stepped inside the unlocked door, through ratted spider
webs. The whitewashed wood was pocked with dirt, a single
window glazed in dust. Behind the altar was a painting of the
Virgin Mary. The only other furnishings were a single pew and
a cross.

The air was stifling but the room was bright in a way that
seemed soothing and pristine. She sat in the pew and flipped
through a weathered Bible. She put it down again and folded
her hands in her lap.

She had tried once or twice to go to church in the city. The
only place she had liked was the Spanish mission, not a church
but a museum, with its white adobe walls and frescoes, its plain,
uncarved wood. She especially loved the dioramas of peaceful
mission life, contented Indians feeding cows and planting corn,

beneficent-looking Franciscans, the small DO NOT TOUCH signs all around. But every time she left, the transition to daylight, the brown palm fronds rotting in the median outside, the diorama figures and the Christ on the cross far away like childhood dolls, and she realized all over again, unbearably, the hours to go until sunset. So she'd stopped going to the mission too.

The brightness and calm of the chapel in the middle of the field made her think it would feel different. The Virgin Mary's beatific face not unlike the teller's. Like that of a confidante B. had yet to make. She knelt down on the *prie-dieu*, clasped her hands together, looked hopefully at the Virgin.

But as she prayed—for help with the carsickness, for guidance in the valley—the spinning returned violently. The hot unmoved air smothering her. She gripped the edge of the pew.

It had been a mistake to stop.

When she sat back in the car the ice cream was a sickly dull puddle in the carton. She pulled over and dumped it in a ditch and drove on.

14.

THE BEAUTY PARLOR THE TELLER recommended was on the main street of the next river town, a sign shaped like a woman's bust in profile. Inside were four barber chairs, two occupied by white-haired ladies. One had already been set with curlers, the other was being finished by the single hairdresser in the place.

B. sat on a folding chair near the door. An air-conditioning box sputtered in the corner. This was a better idea, she told herself, better than stopping at the chapel. She watched the hairdresser, a thin woman with sunken cheeks. The hairdresser's own hair did not look well-styled, an attempt for some kind of lift at the crown that only looked like she'd just woken up. Oscillating fans on the counters blew the fine ends off her shoulders, but she seemed no more cooled off.

B. ignored all this. She felt certain the beauty parlors in the valley would be better than in the city, would hold some deeper significance, for their realness, their location among "truer" women. When the hairdresser finished the second woman and put them under the dryers, she approached B.

"I'd like a set, please."

"We do wash-and-set, ma'am."

"But it's already clean."

"We'll have to wet it anyhow."

B. tried not to sound defeated. "Alright, however you'd like."

The valley hairdresser shampooed her quickly, scraping B.'s scalp with her long fingernails, then sat her in front of the mirror and sectioned her hair with the tail of a comb. She rolled each section up into a wire curler and pinned it tightly, until B.'s temples hurt. The hairdresser's extreme thinness, chipped scarlet nails and limp hair made her look older at first, but as B. watched the woman curl and pin she realized they were probably the same age.

When B. had gone with her mother to the beauty parlor as a girl, her mother's stiff handbag had sat on the floor with gloves laid carefully on top. She chatted with the other ladies in the same crests and falls, attuned to some shared rhythm.

And yet B. could not recall what the women spoke of, or how vital these subjects were, or whether these seemed to be the conversations they really wanted.

B. watched the two older women under the dryers. One was thin like the hairdresser, her skin mottled, the bones in her elbows protruding; the other was weighed down by fat that bulged off her torso and arms. Their voices rattled in the vibration of the dryers. B. listened to their conversation, trying to discern a thread that might be illuminating in some way, that might be what she had come for.

"Well that was just it, and so I took it back to the supermarket and showed them the opened carton. Full of lumps! I said, 'I bought this milk yesterday and I'm not leaving without my money back.'"

"And did they give it?"

"Of course they did."

"Well, I like it there. I'm not going to stop going there."

The thin lady harrumphed.

There was a silence. B. waited for something else.

"I saw that greedy yellow bird again," the thin one began. "Damn bird has no business around here, and it keeps showing up in my apple tree, picking at my apples and leaving holes."

"Did you hear me?" she snapped at the other.

"Uh-huh." But the fat woman was drifting off to sleep.

"You think I could get Fred to poison it? You think that's legal?"

B. turned to them, encouraged. "Was it a warbler?" she asked. The hairdresser cupped B.'s skull and forced her face back to the mirror to set another curler. B. settled for the old women's reflection.

"Well, no, it was a thrush, I think," the thin woman said. She eyed B. "Do you know birds?"

"Well, not much really," B. said. "I thought warblers were yellow, though."

"I'm from the city," she added, as if this explained her error. "But I was thinking of staying here."

"Most coastal folks can't take the heat," the fat woman said flatly.

"People usually driving through here to get somewhere else," the thin woman said. "They don't stay."

"I like the heat," B. said. "I think the valley is interesting."

"You one of them hippies? You trying to set up one of them camps or something?"

"Oh no, of course not. I just liked . . . I'm just interested in how you live."

B. waited hopefully for more, but they only stared at her. They resumed a discussion, privately now, murmuring under the whir of the dryers. She watched their lips in the mirror, the deeply cut wrinkles. B.'s own skin pinched from the curlers and pins. A disappointment sank through her. She brushed it off.

"Do you get many young people coming in?" she tried with the hairdresser.

"Same as everywhere," the woman replied. She did not glance toward B. in the mirror, just pulled at her hair, shoving the final pins in. B. stayed quiet. She watched the hairdresser's half-red nails flutter like bright frightening insects over her head.

Her mother had become increasingly disturbed lately by shades of nail polish. "I'd rather see the white than nothing at all, I suppose," she'd explain to B. "But the yellow is horrible. Clown colors, Easter egg colors. Better nude than colors like that." Her mother had begun calling her often that rainless winter, a creamy haze swallowing the city and her mother phoning almost daily. That January the "human be-in" had happened in the park and her mother seemed obsessed by it.

"The woman with the floppy hat . . . she was in *The Globe* . . . She looked so strange, you know. Dirty. I thought I should call you."

B. had seen the posters around the city—a man with a pyramid and third eye at his forehead, long tangled hair, his face vaguely, eerily African—and she'd seen the pictures in the newspaper, the thousands of bodies standing and dancing and the rock-and-roll bands and flowers and long hair everywhere. B. was disturbed by the be-in too, but all the chatter about it made her more uneasy; as if the more they talked about it, the more portentous it grew. But her mother did not let up.

"Well, she looked ridiculous in that hat. And her hair was the same color as yours, did you realize that?"

"But the photo was black-and-white."

"No, it was the exact same color, I could tell. So I just wanted to call."

"I didn't go. I wasn't there."

Her mother pretended not to hear. She moved on to whom B. had seen that week, what she'd done. After that B. began to let the phone ring without answering.

The hairdresser finished the last of the pins and put B. under a dryer next to the now-sleeping women. Close up the thin old woman's hands were coiled with veins and brown spots like a series of stains. B. reached for a nearby magazine and flipped through it, but her mind drifted to her mother, the white nail polish, the woman in the floppy hat. She turned a page and there was the first lady again, standing in front of a bed of blue flowers in Washington, D.C. B. studied the photograph: red suit and implacable hair, the sea of blue flowers. She felt calmer.

The dryer heat baked into her cells. She must have dozed off because when she woke her scalp was raw and her hair hard and the white-haired women gone.

"How do you want it styled?" the hairdresser asked.

"I'm not really going anywhere."

The hairdresser looked piqued. "However you think best," B. tried to add. But the woman started yanking out the curlers in silence. B. tried not to flinch. She felt silly to have come to the valley parlor at all.

Just then a girl came in. She was perhaps twenty, naturally blonde hair falling to her shoulders. B. felt as though she had not seen a person this girl's age in a beauty parlor in years. She was wearing shorts and a baby-doll halter that showed her midriff. B.'s mood brightened.

"Hiya, Trudy. You have time for me?"

"Sure, Kat. Just let me finish this lady. Up or down today?"

"Down. Most definitely *down*."

The girl plopped into the barber chair next to B. She was not exactly pretty, but had the firmness of youth to her skin, a tight and tan body. She wore heavy makeup, thick pancake shining slightly in the heat, pale blue eye shadow with black eyeliner and thick, black mascara, which made her eyes look small and bruised.

The girl was examining her various profiles in the mirror. "He'll ask me now, Trudy," she said. "It's for sure."

"I don't see why not," the hairdresser responded, but her tone was noncommittal, as if she had visited this conversation before and used up the requisite energy.

"His daddy'll just have to park it," the girl went on, biting her thumbnail in between sentences, still glancing sidelong at her reflection. Then she turned straight on in the mirror. "I'm tired of all the judgments, you know? Sick and tired." The thumbnail went back into her mouth.

"We'll fix you up, hon," the hairdresser said without enthusiasm.

"I like your dress," the girl said abruptly to B.

"Thank you."

"It's from the city, I can tell. Couldn't be from around here. Maybe I'll go to the city for my wedding dress. I'm getting engaged tonight."

The girl turned back to the hairdresser, making pouty lips into the mirror. "Listen, Trudy, I need you to pull out all the stops this time. Totally bitchin', okay?"

The girl's clouded eyes began to haunt B. It was too hard to make out what was behind them. B. rubbed her hands together nervously.

"We do nails, too," the hairdresser said listlessly.

B. glanced down at the rutted pink polish and dug her nails into her lap. "That's alright."

"I'd like to move to the city," the girl said, turning to B. again. "Have our own apartment there. Robby could work in a skyscraper or something. My best friend Debbie was all set to go—you know Deb, don'tcha Trudy?—but she got married last summer and she's already full up with diapers."

"I'm not afraid of the city," the girl added. "My mom thinks it's all druggies and pervs, but I think it'd be boss. Anything to get outta here."

"Oh, well if you want to know anything," B. offered, "I can tell you—"

"—I mean, Robby is going into the Air Force first, and so we'll probably have a house at McClellan to start, but then after he has his pilot's license, we'll go then . . ." Her voice drifted off.

B. did not know why it mattered to her if the girl went to the city or not. And yet she felt betrayed, as if the girl were stranding her by not going to the city. "There are nice beauty parlors in the city," B. murmured. "You might really like them."

"Thing is, it all depends on Mr. Robert R. Taylor *senior*. What a candyass. But he has the money, so it all depends on what he says. I just hope he gets the golf club for the reception.

I just hope he's not too candyass to do that." The girl's eyes were a terrifying smear now, irises and pupils lost in the blue powder and black liner, no reflection at all, calculating opaquely about the golf club for the reception.

"He likes it down, but it's got to be classy. You know, memorable." The girl gnawed on the thumbnail. "Trudes, do you think maybe an updo? Oh, God, if they photograph us at the restaurant, I want a good picture. I want a damn good picture in the paper."

"So you ready for me now?" The girl's bruised eyes pleading. "Trudy?"

The spinning and tightness vibrated in B.'s teeth. She reached for a bank bill to pay and get out and for the first time felt reluctant to part with the money, as if it pulsed out the calm and relief of the banks itself. She forced herself to lay it down on the counter.

The hairdresser did not even notice. The girl was still pleading with her. "God knows I've waited—right, Trudy? No one's waited as long as I have."

B. hurried out of the salon. At the end of the block she went into a columned stone building and came out again. She put the three hundred dollars in her purse. The plaguing voice vanished. She left the windows down in the Mustang and let her new curls fly.

15.

THE NEXT TOWN B. CAME on was the largest she'd seen in the valley. She avoided for a while anything but the fields, driving straight through the flat green and the flat yellow, concentrating on the line in the road. The town appeared from out of nowhere, like an oasis. (Or was she farther south in the valley than she'd thought? She was no longer exactly sure where she was.) The milky blue sky beat down on its empty streets. A few tall palms listed over the main drag, a movie theater with missing letters in its marquee and a church and a Woolworth's. A sign pointed toward a river, the existence of which seemed doubtful in the heat.

She turned down the streets until she came accidentally into a neighborhood. A collection of small one-story cottages. Each yard seemed carefully planted, with gladioli and rose bushes, geraniums and fuchsia. Actual trees, a rare collection, stooped over the houses. There was a quietness about the place. Everything seemed quaint and tidy and protected. She parked the car and got out.

She walked up the block. At a cream-colored stucco house she walked up to the arched window. The entire living room was visible. She stood in the shade of a magnolia tree and peered in at a dark green couch and dark green armchair, both decorated with antimacassars at the heads and arms. In the corner of the room a black-and-white television was on. On the dark dining room table she could see a stack of envelopes and a thick book whose title she could not make out. There was a large crucifix in the center of one wall, two small ceramic angels around it. She waited to discern something, some message or communication from these choices, this arrangement. The beauty parlor girl's blue-and-black smears and the old thin woman's mottled hands flashed at her. She moved to a different part of the window and continued to watch.

B. waited for someone to come into the front room. For a split second she saw her reflection in the window, the curls wind-ragged, her shoulders pink. The reflection seemed far away; it was the image of a disheveled thin woman. She waited for someone to turn off the television and its flickering gray images. No one came.

She stood there she was not sure how long until she noticed a different reflection. A mailman watching from across the street. She raised her hand to wave. He did not wave back.

Finally she walked back to the Mustang. She sat at the wheel. The television images from the stucco house flitted in front of her: a woman with a box of laundry detergent; a man with a briefcase; a woman in an evening dress. She tried to put these images together in illustration of something, a code to the house, to its way of life.

She did not notice the police officer until he was knocking on the window. The sun was angled low behind him, blurring his outline. She rolled the window down.

"Oh, I'm sorry," she said. "Is there something wrong?"

"Do you have a license, ma'am?"

"Of course." She reached over to her purse on the passenger seat. There was a stain from the ice cream on the floorboard; she hoped the police officer could not see it. She drew out her wallet, trying not to open the purse too wide to reveal the fifty-dollar bills.

"I was just feeling tired. They say it's better not to drive when you're tired."

He studied her license. Her face flushed; how closely would he look at it? His fingers around it were large and ruddy, big blond hair follicles in the knuckles. He stooped to her eye level, elbow in the door.

"You're a ways from the city."

She made herself observe his badge, his holster. "I'm meeting a friend in Reno, and I was just stopping to do an errand and I wanted to see the neighborhood, and . . . it's such a nice-seeming neighborhood . . . then I realized I was a little tired."

He peered down at the license again, then at her. He could not, she reminded herself, know about the checkbook. Or the bills. Then she realized from the way his gaze returned to her and darted shyly over her face that he was finding her attractive. She had learned she must respond to these cues, that to do so put her at an advantage in a situation.

She brushed a strand of hair out of her eyes. "Maybe I should get a cup of coffee," she said, biting her lip. "Could you recommend a place?"

The officer coughed. "Well, there's a Sambo's at Second and Main. Just take a right here and go about five blocks."

"Thank you."

He hesitated and cleared his throat. "Try not to let someone find you like this again."

"Yes, sir. Thank you."

The houses looked gilded and soft in the late light; she did not want to leave them. But the policeman would not start his squad car until she started the Mustang, after which he followed. Her shoulders tensed until finally he turned.

The Sambo's was a bright orange color outside, the booths and light fixtures the same lurid orange inside. The theme of the restaurant unfolded in a vaguely disturbing cartoon along the walls, in which a tiger was turned into butter as punishment for trying to eat a child. But the melted butter did make one think of pancakes, B. thought, and she ordered a stack and coffee.

Things were happening that B. had not intended. She had not intended to stand on a lawn looking into someone else's picture window in broad daylight. She had not intended to present a fake license to a police officer. She should, she knew, stop to consider these events. Ascertain some schema to them, formulate a plan in reaction. But she sensed for the first time that something dire might occur if she stopped to do this, if she stopped to examine any of it. What was so terrible about wanting to move forward? she thought.

Cheered by this slant on things and the coffee, B. borrowed a pen from the waitress and began sketching on a napkin the stucco house and the dining room table. When her pancakes came, she noticed a girl sitting alone in a corner booth, also writing, in a notebook. The girl sat with a cup of coffee and a few balled-up dollar bills, a large knapsack at her feet. It was unclear whether she'd eaten or not. Her skin was deeply tanned, her long hair falling in greasy sections to the table. She wore fraying blue jeans, dirty at the hems, a loose peasant blouse, and a choker made of leather. Her feet were bare. She seemed like a brown and wind-tangled child just come in from the beach, except for the frown lines in her forehead and the shadows under her eyes.

"I'd appreciate it oh so much if I could get more coffee the same as everyone else," the girl said to the waitress, who seemed to be ignoring her. "Jesus Christ. You'd think I wasn't *paying*."

A *LIFE* magazine protruded from underneath the girl's knapsack; she ran her toes back and forth over the gloss. B. had seen the cover everywhere in the spring: the bride in a mushroom cloud of white veil, cascading white and yellow roses, the groom's hair slicked carefully to the side, ascot gray and black. The young senator's daughter and the young wealthy family's son. A picture making all the sense in the world.

Except that after the cover appeared, B. had begun having the same dream. Her graduation luncheon, the white-linened tables and camellias in glass bowls, the early humidity glazing her face. (The yellow dress her mother had insisted on to complement her hair sometimes lavender, sometimes blue.) What upset her in the dream was that the speech was never intelligible. The Rotarian's or Junior Leaguer's or fundraising committee chair's words always cut off by a faint high-pitched scream, a terrified animal shriek B. imagined might occur during a stabbing or a rape. What came through made no sense: "Take the higher road . . . gentle abiding . . . look happy, now . . ." What could it mean?

B. woke from these dreams with her nightgown sweat through.

The girl arranged sugar packets in a circle on the table. She seemed engrossed in getting the white packets to curve out smoothly, widening larger and larger until she ran out. The waitress returned and said something under her breath, not refilling the girl's cup, and at that moment the girl casually swept her arm across the table and dropped all the sugar packets onto the floor.

B. gaped at the scattered packets.

"You should pick those up." She had not meant to say it out loud.

"Why?"

The girl seemed to look right through her. The blank stare frightened B. She jumped up from her booth, knocking over the silverware, trying to get out. On the way to the register she dropped her purse, the ostrich skin strangely flesh-like against the orange-flecked linoleum, her lipstick rolling onto the floor, the checkbook slipping out. B. scrambled to gather them and pay. Outside, the air was still hot and dry. The town in the dusk looked even more empty. She walked quickly down a few blocks, the white packets raining on the floor and the girl's sullen blank eyes on her, and when she passed underneath a decorative Spanish arch, there was only the same empty street on the other side.

16.

THE NEXT MORNING, IN THE motel bed, she fingered the collar of the powder-blue dress. She had not meant to sleep in it. There was a coffee stain at her breast and a pungent dampness under her arms. The night before she'd had the intention of washing her underthings. She'd laid out her bra and panties next to the sink and found her Woolite travel packets. Then she'd sat on the bed and the intention had lost its keenness. She must have lain down.

The already-warm morning air smelled faintly of green onion. (There was a kind of onion grass wasn't there? Did it resemble chives? The question nagged her.) She watched the line of blue sky through the curtain. It made her think of the sky through the magnolia trees from the day before. The cottages shared the same compactness of the lake house, the same shade and light, she thought. She had lost something in the lake house. She lay in the motel bed contemplating the line of blue sky and what it was she had missed, but she could not grasp it.

When she got up from the bed finally, she smoothed down her hair, limp from the over-washing and wind. She wiped the makeup from under her eyes and applied new lipstick and mascara.

She made sure the bills were tucked into her purse and left the Mustang in the motel parking lot to walk toward the center of the town. It was early, so she stopped in a small park and sat on a bench. The freshly mown grass shone darkly from sprinklers. An old man sat at the other end of the park feeding bread to small brown birds. B. imagined herself coming here to read or picnic. She thought perhaps she could even be like the old man, quiet and serene tossing crumbs of bread.

But a sense of pale familiarity descended on her. Why would the park be any different from the ones in the city? What would she tell people she was doing there? Her head spun. She rose from the bench and walked across the lawn, pieces of wet grass sticking to the bone-colored heels, and tried to calm her breathing. The old man's birds took flight. She walked past the main street, to the river, low and brown. The onion smell had evaporated, the heat of the day already inescapable. She walked along the river until her breathing evened and the spinning slightly lessened.

She found the real estate office. It was a storefront with a few photos of houses in the window. A woman sat at a desk flipping through papers. She had styled, shoulder-length hair and a tan dress belted at the hips. She studied B. for a beat before she smiled.

"Can I help you?"

"I'd like to look at houses for sale in the area."

The woman lowered her reading glasses to her nose and scanned B. "Are you visiting from the city?"

"Do you have time to show me anything?"

The woman hesitated. "I can take you round a couple places, although I find it helpful to have both of you along, to ask questions, get things clear," she said. "Should we wait for anyone?"

"No. I'm ready to go now."

Again the woman studied B. and seemed after a moment to make some assessment that allowed her to stand up from her desk.

"I'll drive us out."

They walked to the woman's car in back, the steering wheel and dashboard, seats and doors of which were lined in an immaculate white calfskin. B. hesitated to sit on it. The woman warmed up once they were in the car. "My husband and I were both planning to move to the city, you know, before we met. Funny how life works out. His plans fell through, and so did mine, and otherwise we would never have met.

"I still love to visit, though," the woman went on. "Seeing

the bay is a thrill. Although I'm not sure these days it's the safest place." She hmmmed in agreement with her own observation.

"It's a small town, but our schools are good, and we have strong clubs and community groups. It's right to get out of the city, I think, once you've decided." Her voice fell into a con-spiratorial tone. "I know how hard it is to get them to stop thinking big big big, to stop them wanting to be in the game. It's something caveman-ish in them, I think. Ronald still talks about moving to the city—at thirty-seven! Thinking they have to be where the action is. But if you can steer the boat the right way, it's the best thing."

B. knew she was expected to offer some personal story here, some hint of her plan, but she said nothing, watching the faded stores and buildings pass by.

The woman eyed B. "Do you think you'll be starting a family soon? These are the kinds of things it's best for me to know, so you don't settle in and find out you need a nursery."

"I'd rather just see something first."

"Suit yourself. I've only been in real estate for thirteen years."

They were on the highway now, alongside a line of sharp-edged pink and white oleander, and suddenly the town was behind them and they were back in the fields. It was a devel-opment, with a main artery and small streets shooting off, low beige mirror-image houses and thin new trees around the perimeter. Each had a new lawn and a two-car garage and, B. imagined, a swimming pool out back.

"It's not what I want," B. blurted out.

The realtor was listing the amenities of the houses, ". . . new double ovens, sunken living rooms, automatic garage doors . . ."

"I was in a neighborhood last night near your office," B. said. "That's where I want to go. Take me back."

"Downtown? That's old folks. Retirees and widowers on their own." The realtor grimaced. "Don't you even want to go inside one of the new ones?"

"Take me back now, please. That's where I want to look."

The woman scowled. Her fingers gripped the white calfskin of the steering wheel so hard B. was afraid she might soil it. She turned the car around in one of the new driveways. "Those houses are too small, you realize, not in any condition," she said. "Really, they're falling apart inside. Not suitable for families at all."

As they drove back along the sharp oleander the lake house descended on B. again. She had the feeling whatever she had lost there she could get back in one of the old cottages. A desperation climbed through her to get to the cottages; she braced herself against the blaring white seat. *Hurry*, she thought, *hurry*. As they drove, she tried to calm herself with images of new curtains and a divan on which to read her books, a cookbook with recipes for fingerling potatoes and roasts, a sewing machine maybe. It seemed so simple.

"There's only one I agreed to show," the realtor was saying. "I felt sorry for the children, you know, trying to move on with

their lives. The father eating out of tin cans at the end, for pity's
sake." They parked in front of a white wooden cottage with
green trim and one of the large magnolias in front. Its suede leaves
littered the dry lawn. The realtor led her up to the front door. B.
tried to ignore a pang of disappointment at the chipped paint and
the rusted knocker. The house was empty. The realtor shuttled
her through the rooms, with square pale outlines on the walls
of picture frames removed. "No dishwasher, no central air,
no electric stove, here's the one closet you would share . . ."
B. tried to rally herself by visualizing the bookshelves she
could stain herself, the new curtains she could learn to sew.
But her heart sank at the cracked porcelain sinks and the split-
ting baseboards. She thought inexplicably of the girl's dirty bare
feet on the magazine cover in the Sambo's. "Could you show
me another?" she asked the realtor. "Nothing else is up in this
neighborhood," the woman said stonily. "That's what I've been
trying to tell you. People stay until they die. They've been in
there since their honeymoons, since the war." She sighed. B. left
her and walked back to the front yard. The houses all at once
looked dilapidated, gardens dying. What had she been thinking?
She couldn't buy a house on her own; she couldn't fix it up. The
tightening seized her neck and head. The pale washed-out park
of the morning hung before her. She saw that it was a version
of every park she'd ever seen before, would ever see again. She
bent over and brought her hand to her stomach and dry-heaved.
She could not move from the dead lawn. Like a day in the city

when she'd frozen in the middle of an intersection, immobile, realizing there was nowhere to go—backward, forward, it was all the same. The traffic light changing and the cars honking as she stared at a crumpled bus transfer, until a man stepped out and pulled her to the curb.

Through the haze of this memory, the realtor was making squawking sounds like a crow. Demanding to know where B. was staying, how she had gotten there, if she was going to be sick. When B. understood this last question she wanted to tell the woman that she was not, that if she could be sick, it might be better.

"I'm sorry but I can't help someone in your condition." The squawking now arranging itself into sentences. "I try and keep up with the times. I like the city. But we're different out here. We have morals. It was strange enough that you were alone, but now . . ." An objection formed in B.'s mind, but she could not get it out of her mouth. Before she knew it, she was back inside the spotless calfskin and then deposited in the motel parking lot, waves of heat shimmering off the asphalt. A car door slammed and the realtor was gone and B. stood beside the Mustang, the blue metal searing.

She stumbled into her room and gathered her travel bag, leaving the Woolite packets, and left cash and her room key in the office. Her shoulders contracted into each other, her head spiraled. She climbed in the Mustang and exited the motel parking lot without any sensation of movement.

The one she found was new. A rectangular building finished in concrete. Carpet on the floors, blinds on the windows, all the furniture an approximation of dark wood. But the same innocuous, soothing tones, the same calm safe lines. She stood for a moment near the door, just breathing. She approached the island with deposit and withdrawal slips, ran her hand back and forth along the smooth counter until it steadied and filled out one of the slips.

She heard herself making small talk—about the heat, about the girl's birthstone ring ("Topaz, it has healing powers. I would invest in some, Sag or not.")—watched the girl stamp the check and place it in a drawer and deal out the cash. She stood there as the light softened, the blue veins in the teller's neck receded, the sallow skin under the girl's dyed-black hair pinkened, the spinning stopped.

But when she climbed back into the Mustang, the town was like a maze. She circled the surface streets without finding the highway. She passed the same liquor store twice, two old sunburned men outside, leering at her, she thought. The tight pulse returned behind her eyes. It had never come back so quickly. She sped up but the tightening only increased. She couldn't stand it; she turned the car around. When she reached the bank she stepped in and sat on one of the hard settees, clutching the ostrich-skin purse.

"Did you need something else?" The teller was beside her, smiling with a ghostly white lipstick B. had not noticed the first time. "I'm going on my break."

"No, I'm sorry. I just . . . I was a bit lost . . . I'm not sure . . ." B. zeroed in on the girl's teeth. They were small and straight and attractive. She looked from the teeth to the clean desks to the beige-colored carpet.

"We probably have a map here somewhere."

"No. I just need to rest. Thank you." She spoke very slowly to the teeth.

The girl nodded sympathetically, but B. picked up in a corner of her eye the silver badge and white shirt of the security guard.

"It's nice and cool in here," the girl said, nodding. "It can get outta sight, especially for someone from the city. Would you like a glass of water?"

"No, really, I'm fine. Thank you." The teeth and the lines and the orderliness doing their work now. The cool expansive feeling returning, her pulse relaxing.

"Well, take your time. And thank you for banking Delta Savings and Loan."

After the teller walked away, B. saw the security guard still watching her. She waited a few moments before she stood up, leaning against the slick beige wall. She exited as casually as possible out the glass door, the cool expansiveness pouring through her. She sat for a few more seconds in the car, noting the silver badge glinting behind the glass. This time she drove carefully, following the main street straight to the highway. Then she gunned the engine, eye on the rearview mirror.

17.

AT ONE TIME B. HAD wondered whether marriage was the way things would "work out." The girls at her small women's college had come to find husbands; a few had ambitions for publishing jobs or teaching positions, but most came for a ring or a promise, and sometimes they deliberately got pregnant. B. had not railed against or even chafed at this reality. It had seemed an acceptable fact. But remote, like growing old, something she could navigate later. She'd simply enjoyed reading her textbooks, about floral imagery in Japanese art or the brutal deaths of Roman emperors. She dated a few boys from the men's college, all perfectly fine, but the prospect of the dates always seemed more entertaining for her roommates, who dressed her and fixed her makeup and hair and talked about the boy's height or skin and told bawdy jokes about penises. B. liked to be touched and kissed by the young men but she did not feel in their brief interludes particularly engrossed by them. She could never overcome, the way her classmates seemed able to, her discomfort at the gap between what she was thinking and what she was supposed to say. (A boy had once told her "You seem like a real fun girl" at the exact moment she had been wondering whether Bloody Queen Mary of Scots still had feeling in her neck between the first and second hacks; she'd nodded to the boy, not wanting to embarrass him.) One boy wanted to see her often. They had a date at a soda counter and one at a movie where his large knee brushing hers made her groin surge; they kissed for long periods. After a few more dates no different than these, the boy proposed. He did not seem bothered by the fact that they had spoken probably an hour total to each other, that he had no idea what she'd really thought of the movie (sentimental) or why she typically avoided soda counters (a tendency to spill). She lied that she was already engaged and the boy had called her heartless. She'd watched his slumped shoulders with relief as he walked away.

But a few years later, living in Boston and working as a secretary, no longer studying Japanese art or Roman emperors or thinking about Bloody Queen Mary of Scots, B. wondered if the presence of another person every day could keep away the tightening and spinning in her skull. She looked up the boy who'd proposed and invited him for a drink. They saw each other for several weeks, but each night after he fell asleep the carsickness resurfaced as it had before, the boy's warm and prone body like an island unto itself, and she reeled in the dark. She broke it off with him again and this time he spat at her. After that she no longer wondered if marriage was the answer.

And so it had all become a haunting, really, the idea of things "working out." As if she were missing the other half of a position. As if she had gotten herself to a ledge with no intention of leaping off.

18.

ON THE MAP FROM THE gas station, they were a few jagged circles alone, disconnected. She took the freeway in her hurry to get there.

It was private land, she understood. She would not be allowed to drive in the buttes. But she felt suddenly desperate to see their desultoriness up close. Geological anomalies, mountains in the middle of a valley. She felt some aspect of them must elucidate something, must point her in a direction.

To her right the shoulder was a streak of yellow grass dotted with trash. On and on, unvarying. Still, in this unending line, B. found herself waiting for something to appear. How could she be waiting? There was no sign that anything but the line of yellow grass would continue. This waiting, she sensed, was part of the problem. The feeling that if she just waited, somehow things would be resolved. Descend on her, materialize, make themselves clear. She felt programmed for it, she realized, as if to wait had been implanted in her body before she was born.

She sped up the car.

A crew of orange-vested men flashed by in the yellow line, picking up the trash. The blip of their faces pained in the heat. On another stretch the thump of a dead animal. The freeway streaming on. In her head a nursery rhyme drummed: *Seventeen, eighteen, maids in waiting.*

Her eyes watered from the smog. She rolled up her window. She reached out to touch the checkbook, but the ostrich-skin purse was on the floorboard out of reach.

The buttes when they finally rose in her windshield were ugly. Mounts of yellow brown in the haze, bare land with a few shrubs and oaks in its crevices. She drove on, determined. She reached the base and pulled onto a dirt road. At a locked gate not far in she parked. She got out; the dead engine pinged. At the gate, she climbed awkwardly over in her dress, stumbling in her heels as she jumped down. She followed along barbed wire, the hillside smelling of dry mustard and dust.

The sun blazed down. There were no buildings anywhere. Bits of trash from other trespassers, a beer bottle, silver pull tabs, crumpled brown bags. The silver tabs were flashing a message maybe. *Thirteen, fourteen, maids a-courting, fifteen, sixteen, maids in the kitchen.* She watched the tabs, then gave up and walked on.

She left the road and began hiking up the hillside. There was "chaparral"—this one classification of tangled green bushes so foreign to her when she came west that she'd had to learn the name—and oak trees scattered and stooping. The powder-blue dress chafed at her underarms. Her heels were blistering. She took off the shoes. The dead grass and rocks pricked her feet but she could not put her throbbing soles back in the heels.

She felt whatever she was looking for must be farther on.

The top was not far. The sun fell in one pure burn into her skin. Finally she collapsed under one of the oaks, throat dry, too hot to continue. The flatness of the valley spread for hundreds of miles below, the mountains in the far distance like figments behind the haze. She could not make out any message, no revelation in any of it. She leaned against the tree. The feeling of solitude, at least, was pleasurable. No one would disturb her here. She closed her eyes.

In her mind, two women swirled. The first from a party, the only contact she'd had with "the scene." A man in line at the supermarket had asked B. whether the grapes in her basket were picked by Mexican migrant workers, and when she could not say they hadn't been, he'd begun declaiming about seasonal labor movements and the exploitation of brown-skinned "proles" by capitalist dictators ("in this so-called 'democratic' society") and then asked her to coffee. He had a wisp of awful breath and a slight droop to his left eye. Perhaps out of curiosity, or to occupy the hours, as with Daughtry, she'd accepted. When they met he did not ask her thoughts on anything. He listed his work in the service of the poor and downtrodden and disdained the "bourgeois café" where he had suggested they meet. He invited her to a party. The breath was worse, of a person who never flossed, whose teeth held rotting pieces of food. But she thought of the basement apartment and the long weekend ahead and again she accepted.

The party was in a run-down Victorian in the neighborhood where the young people flocked. Stairs led to a railroad flat with fewer people than B. had imagined, a phonograph playing a rock band she did not know, one sagging couch. Pages from books were taped to the wall, a Dylan Thomas poem, an illustration of what she guessed from the many arms and blue skin was some Hindu god, an astrological chart over a dying, half-brown ficus in the corner. Her date left to talk to friends and a woman near the liquor table handed B. a paper cup of wine and began asking her whether she understood that an orgasm was a basic human right. "I mean like food and oxygen," the woman clarified. She demanded to know whether B. let strangers call her by her first name. "They do it at the doctor's office, the dry cleaner's, and you need to *tell* them. Instruct them. 'It's *Miss Smith*, thank you.' I mean, would they call a man by his first name?" The woman glowered, seemingly at the dry cleaners and grocery men in her mind. "It's the insidious shit that keeps us down."

Her voice began stirring up the carsickness. B. drank more wine. But the tight spinning at the back of her neck seemed to coat the room and yellow the walls. B. excused herself to the bathroom to escape and wandered into a dark hallway that seemed to go on forever. At the end of it was a woman. She sat in the dark on the floor, wearing, B. could just make out, a short dress the weight of a handkerchief, with African-looking patterns and a deep V in front showing her nipples; her hair went past her shoulders, her sandals snaked up her legs. She did not move at B.'s approach. Her trance was total, her head tilted back, her eyes rolling under their lids. B. understood from all these signs that the woman was on a "trip," that she was beyond herself, in another realm. B. had no interest in acid. But she could not stop watching the woman. She would have reached out to touch her, to ask for her advice somehow, to look into her eyes—perhaps help her cover the nipples—if B.'s date had not found her, with his sulfurous breath and another story about organizing the workers (to which B. asked if he spoke Spanish and to which he'd replied that this was beside the point). He led her back into the party and B. lost the woman in the dark.

The other woman swirling in her mind was dead. B. had heard about it from one of the secretaries: the woman had been running across the street—her hair and nails clearly just done, the cherry red polish shining brightly in the sunlight—and then she had gone up and over the hood of a car and onto the ground. Her grocery bag torn and a wine bottle staining the asphalt and freshly cut daisies shivering in blood. All of which details B. saw vividly in her mind, the secretary having mentioned none of them. B. remembered thinking at the time that this woman had probably felt everything was "working out." She'd bought the wine and picked the flowers and manicured her nails. And B. had felt a strange relief for her.

She sat like this under the oak tree, her mind confused but soft, the two women swirling, for she did not know how long. The heat dissolved. At some point, the chaparral shivered on the hillside. Stories of mountain lions pierced her trance briefly, but she did not want to move. She felt as if she was just on the other side of something—an answer? a riddle? But the woman from the party frightened her and the woman in the street was dead. There was nothing to put together. She grazed her fingernails back and forth in the dirt.

When the chaparral below her rustled again, she forced herself up. She climbed higher through the hard dirt and dried grass. She looked back for the mountain lion and at that moment stabbed the sole of her foot. The piece of glass was partway in. She removed it. She limped along without stopping. The top of the buttes was too near.

When she got there, it felt as if she were in one of the banks. The silence and remove, the calm and peace. A pleasant cloudiness spread through her, making nothing particular about her in that moment, everything fluid and easy to deflect; no stories, no afflictions; she was only a vapor. Her foot stung, her mouth gluey, the sun burning directly on her scalp. A trickle of blood ran from her foot; the cut was marbled with dirt. And yet in this moment above the pink smogged air, she could occlude from her mind further thoughts about waiting, marriage, about things "working out," about the drugged woman at the party and the dead woman in the street. She thought vaguely she must get a bandage. She thought vaguely, I'd like to sleep here. It was only the idea of the mountain lion that kept her from lying down in the dirt and dead grass to stay. Finally, after an hour or so, she forced herself to go down again the way she'd come, limping on the side of her foot.

Something on the way down glinted in the sun. A pocket knife in the grass, the blade open. She could not think why it would be there. She picked it up and took it with her. Her mind was already losing its relaxedness, the pleasant cloudiness dissipating. Thoughts began to crowd her again . . . *Seventeen, eighteen, maids a-waiting* . . . She walked faster. The cut brushed on each step.

By the time she came back to the Mustang, the sun was coming down the western half of the sky. Her feet and hands were filthy, her face and shoulders red. Flies buzzed her neck. In the car, she tore a piece of the map and wiped away the blood and wrapped the paper around her foot. She put the heels back on. When she tilted the rearview, there was a streak of dust across her chest and a fingerprint of blood at her collar bone. She tilted the mirror away and drove.

She drove south. Huge trucks barreled by her on the freeway. She was light-headed from hunger and thirst. She stopped at a taco stand off an exit ramp. A small Mexican man stood at a window in the side of a trailer, a short heavyset woman behind him at a grill. There was no shade anywhere as the late afternoon sun bore down on them. The smell of onions and sizzling pork made B. momentarily sick. She braced herself against the counter. The woman handed her a paper cup of water. "You alright, ma'am?" B. gulped it down and nodded, trying to smile. She ordered a taco and an orange soda. There was a third Mexican leaning on the trailer, chatting with the cook in Spanish. He was laughing and B. saw him look at her feet, the torn map, her dress. When the taco was ready, she went back to the Mustang although it was stifling inside. She gulped down the soda in one pull. She took a few bites of the taco but nausea and dizziness made her stop and she wrapped it back in its tinfoil and put it on the floor. She lay across her seats for a moment, trying to push through the dizziness.

She never should have left the buttes, she thought.

She made herself rise and start the engine. The light was copper through the car but B. did not notice it. She repeated to herself the nursery rhyme. Then she repeated to herself to the rhythm of the concrete breaks: *get there, get there, get there.* Her foot throbbed. Images of the realtor and the blue-smeared eyes of the girl returned. And it was not until the sky turned gray and the fields had dimmed that she finally realized: the banks were closed.

19.

WHEN SHE ENTERED THE NEXT town, a college town, there was already a sliver of moon. In the absence of a bank she must get to a motel and lie down, she told herself. But first a bandage. She scanned the streets for a drugstore. Everything deserted, the campus empty. The student-rented houses looked derelict even in the dark, couches on sidewalks, sagging stairs and porches, overgrown straw lawns. She parked the car to find a corner store at least. She walked through the abandoned campus. Crickets buzzed loudly. Her feet were raw in the bone-colored heels, the wound oozing through the paper. She sat on a bench. A few young people passed along the cement paths, in and out of pools of lamplight. The crickets droned on, the air smelled of grass, the night was hot. From nowhere it seemed a man came out of the dark and sat next to her.

"Best time to be here," the man said. "No students."

"It's very quiet."

"Quiet. Obscured."

She did not turn her head to him, in part because she knew she must look terrible, in part because she was afraid to see his face, she did not know why. "I'm trying to find a drugstore," she finally said.

"Are you alright?" He turned toward her then, and she made herself look. He was maybe a decade older than she, but tanned and handsome, thick brown hair that had begun to gray at the temples. She wished she had the energy to take out her compact.

"Yes. My foot is cut a little, that's all."

"Everything's closed now," he said. Dozens of sprinklers exploded on, the jagged arcs thrusting in the dark.

"I have some bandages at my house," the man eventually said. "It's just down across the way there."

"Oh. I don't know . . ."

"I'm harmless, I promise. You could infect the cut walking on it like that."

She'd seen his wedding ring, wide and shiny. He spoke in a slow liquid manner, possibly from drinking, she thought. But a quality in his voice was reassuringly authoritative (he must be a professor, she decided); she felt too tired to argue.

"Alright. Thank you."

She put back on her heels. They walked along one of the

paths, the sprinklers catching their ankles. The house, oppo-
site the quad, was a small Craftsman with every light on. The
woodwork inside was mahogany, the ceilings low and the walls
crowded with bookshelves, a comforting feel, although she
wished the blazing lights would go away. B. noticed various
charcoal sketches on the walls of nude women with giant
engorged nipples. In one corner a tall heavy African mask.
Piles of papers scattered across the tables and chairs.

He led her into the bathroom. There was a shaving kit open
on a shelf, a can of woman's hairspray and an open jar of cold
cream, as if two people were still in the midst of getting ready.
The man motioned her to sit on the side of the tub and ran the
water until it was warm, then bent down next to her and washed
her hands, then her feet. She smelled the man's aftershave and
the liquor on his breath; his tanned hands on her skin briefly
made her stiffen. The white washcloth turned brown with dirt;
B. blushed, embarrassed. When her foot was washed he moved
her to the toilet seat and swabbed the cut with antiseptic, then
reached for her dress and picked off a few spurs. B. waited for
him to finish with gauze and tape for her foot but he stood up
and put everything away.

"Shouldn't it be bandaged?"

"No. It needs to develop a protective layer. Open air."

"Stay for a drink," he added.

He left the bathroom before she could respond and she hob-
bled behind him on the side of her foot. She realized then a

radio had been on, beating out a twisting, low and mournful jazz that made the house drowsy. She sat down on a couch next to more papers.

"You don't live around here," he said, handing her a glass.

"No. Visiting." She thought briefly she should not be drinking with a stranger, she should get back on the road and find a motel. But the tiredness and light-headedness (did she have a bit of sunstroke?) made her unable to move.

"And why on earth, dear lady, would you visit Chico? You have an Aunt Alma here or some other bad luck?"

"No, I've just been driving." She did not feel like knitting together the explanation in her mind. She drank her scotch.

"We haven't been here long," the man said. "Still finishing the dissertation. We're out from New York. That's where my wife is now. That faraway galaxy called New York . . ." He peered dolefully into his drink.

"I'm from the East too."

He did not seem to hear her. "So you're really just driving? No obligations, no appointments? Sounds lawless."

She fidgeted. Some of the papers from the couch fell onto the floor. She bent to pick them up.

"Don't bother about those. No point."

"Does your wife like it out here?"

"Oh, she's busy enough keeping me in line, you know." He laughed but it was not cheery. He fiddled with a thread on the arm of his chair. "It's been an adjustment for her, cooking more, keeping up a house instead of an apartment. I mean, she paints and sketches too, of course." He pointed at the charcoals.

The drawings troubled B. She tried to find them modern, but the nipples were out of proportion, bellicose. "They're very interesting," she said.

"How old are you?"

Suddenly a chorus of drunk voices crowded in through the windows. "Well, helloooo, Professor! Helloooo, helloooo! Another one of your 'conferences'?" Howls of laughter, catcalls.

The man raised his hand in embarrassed greeting. It was impossible with all the lights to make out any faces in the dark.

"Don't give that grade 'til she earns it!" someone yelled, then more howls of laughter. The man's face looked like it would turn red if it weren't so mellowed. A few more mutterings and hoots and the commotion faded out.

"The frats stay here all summer," he explained. "Amazing they survive to fall."

"Thirty."

"Pardon?"

"I'm thirty years old."

He looked her up and down. "Well. What a nice change. I'm usually in the company of nubile student-girls—severely off-limits, of course—or mommies and widows." He got up and went into the kitchen. She heard the slamming of cabinets and the suction of a freezer door, ice clinking.

When he came back, he held a refilled drink in one hand

and the bottle in the other. He sat back across from her in the slouchy arm chair, tearing more thread out of the upholstery, widening the hole. "*I saw pale kings, and princes too,/Pale warriors, death-pale were they all;/They cried—'La belle Dame sans merci/ Hath thee in thrall!'* You made me think of that. Keats. My dissertation."

"Well, thank you . . . I think . . . It's lovely."

"What I find lovely, and fascinating, is exactly what a thirty-year-old woman is doing driving around the valley for no reason."

"It's not for no reason."

"No?"

The lights felt momentarily blinding. She drank more scotch. "Can you turn some of the lights off, please? I have a bit of a headache."

"Whatever the lady wants." He walked around the room and hallway until all the lights were off except a small lamp on an end table. She picked at a stain on her dress, hoping he would drop the subject.

"It's funny," he went on, "I find I can talk more easily to single women of a certain age. I tend to go out of bounds. Not always appreciated in normal, civilized speak. I've found that mature-yet-not-coarsened sensibilities appreciate the out-of-bounds from time to time."

"I can't talk to people easily," she said. The dimmed room relaxed her; it might be the alcohol, she realized. "In college I was passable at it, but not anymore . . .

"What do you and your wife talk about, usually?" she asked.

"Ha! That's funny." But he didn't laugh, only drank more.

"No, really."

"Oh, c'mon. We're married. What do married people talk about? You're obviously not married."

She peered into her scotch with a vague irritation. "No."

"In fact, now I'm putting it together," he said, leaning forward, the mellowed face brightening. "Thirty and unmarried. That's it: you're on a quest. A midlife journey. Something mystical even.

"I ran away from the East too," he went on without waiting for corroboration. "Didn't want all that baggage and dusty claptrap. Not to mention the tenure tracks were for the picking out here—forgive the pun. *The days of peace and slumberous calm are fled . . .*"

"I don't really read poetry," B. said.

"Most people don't." He got up to refill their drinks and then sat down beside her on the couch. He stretched an arm out behind her shoulder. She found she didn't mind.

"How old is your wife?" It was the scotch, she realized. The scotch was making her open, calm.

"You're awfully interested in my wife."

"You asked my age."

"Look, let's get to this. What are you, pregnant? A dyke? Wanted by J. Edgar Hoover?"

"I just think it will help." She was suddenly aggravated. "To get away from the city for a while. It's really none of your business anyway."

"I'm sorry," he said. His face filled with what looked like true remorse. "That was wrong of me." He drank down the rest of his glass. "I like a few drinks, honestly. I get uncivilized sometimes. It's why my wife is out east at the moment."

They sat silent.

"Hey, do you know the one about the blonde and the drunk professor? Hilarious. Just wait a few days and I'll remember the punch line."

She smiled.

He stood up, slightly swaying. "We need a bit of dancing, I think." He held out his hand.

She hesitated. But it was all nice, the talking, the drinking, the dimness. She rose and took his hand. They began to shuffle together back and forth clumsily, she on the side of her foot. His smell was richer in the dark. The room swirled around her as they rocked, the books and the *objets d'art* taunting with their French titles and hanging breasts, the burning cities and Jayne Mansfield's decapitated head in the newspapers at their feet.

He murmured in her ear. "Take me with you. Sounds like a good time. I'll be your helmsman." He kissed her wrist.

She thought in a part of her mind that she should not let a married man kiss her. But she liked him breathing in her ear, she liked a handsome professor trying to figure her out.

They danced cheek to cheek (he was not much taller than she

when they stood together), his skin salty, cologned. She felt the
swaying had to do with the room, not their own bodies, it rocked
her into a kind of trance. The carsickness was buried underneath
the layers of scotch. She should drink more often, she thought.

"I played with paper dolls when I was younger," she whispered into his ear. The image appeared to her as they danced: a
dozen ladies' punch-out outfits with tabs on her bedroom floor,
flouncy chartreuses and roses and tangerines. "It was always the
point to see her in something different. One dress grew tiring
and you tried another, and it was pretty for a while, and then
again it was tiring." She paused. "I didn't have any thoughts
about this when I was a girl." He brought her forearm to his
mouth and sucked on it for a moment, his dry lips and rough
tongue spurring on the memory of the dolls. "But now it seems
so disturbing to me. That I would think of the doll with no care
or concern but what new different dress to wear. What did she
do all day? I never thought about it. I never thought about what
her days would be like."

"They were just paper, darling." Now he nuzzled her neck.
"Just dolls."

"But I should have considered . . ." The scotch had gone all
through her body and the kisses tingled on her skin, rippling
inside her. Her thoughts splintered. The jazz was swirling in a
low moaning wail.

"Is your wife ever nauseous?" she asked abruptly.

"Nauseated," he corrected, licking her collarbone. "I wouldn't know, we don't talk about female things." He unzipped the back of her dress. Her back spasmed when his fingers brushed it. He took down her bra straps and cupped her breasts. "No more about her," he whispered.

He moved her to the couch. He emptied the last bit of scotch into their glasses and finished his in a single go. He pressed her back on the couch and began kissing his way down her breasts and onto her stomach. Somewhere again she thought she must stop; he was married. But the sensation of the kissing and the scotch and having confessed about the dolls made her malleable, new. At her navel he stopped as if struck by something. "People don't really talk, you know. The hippies think we're so rotten and bourgeois, and they don't talk any more than we do—communicate, I mean. I mean, what are they really saying to each other with all this 'turn on and groove'? It's all another way to obfuscate. Cover over the void. Just a different language of avoidance."

He seemed to be speaking to an entire room, not B. in particular, but she did not mind. She lay on her back with her eyes closed, her own voice in her head disappearing. She felt he might have sensed this.

"I see the fear in my students' eyes," he went on. "Those guys outside the window just now. They oughtta be scared. There's no way to know they have it right anymore. They may be totally wrong, useless. I have nothing to tell them." He laid his cheek on her breasts. "They see the others living in the parks, getting high and sticking it to the Man, so what are they supposed to think about themselves? What can I tell them? Subconsciously it grinds them. Subconsciously . . ."

B. was soft and serene in her drunkenness now; no spinning anywhere. She stroked his hair. He inched up next to her until their faces touched. It seemed she had left the city and traveled to the valley precisely to find this man.

He took her hand and pushed it down his pants, guiding it back and forth over his penis. "I wish I had some grass for us," he said.

She craned her mouth toward his, rubbing the penis dutifully, losing her rhythm occasionally. "Say more," she murmured.

"About the grass?"

"No, no . . . the other . . ."

"Yeah, baby? You like the talking? Alright then . . . Listen, it's all a wash. The rules they've been setting up this whole time. The rules will never paper over the abyss, never get it out of our heads, and now the holes are showing up. The fraying. But the holes are deep, unfathomable. The expectations are tumbling down. People don't know which way to go. The crybabies yell about ending the war, and they don't see that it doesn't even matter, the whole charade will end in war and famine and misery. Keats said it—nature and youth and suck at the beauty before it rots. The kids get high, wait for the parents to die. Ha!" He laughed at his own rhyme.

It struck B. even in her drunkenness that his disquisition

about non-believing might be just another form of believing, another attempt at "papering over." But the scotch swallowed the validity of this thought. Anyhow, she preferred the sureness of his authoritative voice. She wanted it to keep talking.

"What does your wife think of the war?" she asked.

"This wife obsession is a serious bummer, as our friends would say." He reached for his empty glass on the coffee table and licked the inside rim. "Never enough," he sighed. "To answer your question, my wife does not think about the war. She may give you an opinion but she does not spend any qualitative part of her days pondering it."

"How do you know?"

"Do you think of the war?"

"No."

"Exactly."

"But I might if I wanted to . . . I could." Anger rose up weakly through the alcohol. She wondered momentarily if he'd slipped her something stronger; but this thought departed. She struggled to her elbows and he pushed her back down.

"Look, she's not here, baby, don't worry. She has what she wants. She has her Ivy Leaguer, her little slice of bohemia. She reads Kant and sketches her nudes and irons my shirts and cooks up spaghetti. She likes it all just fine. She doesn't concern herself with every part of the arrangement." He placed B.'s hand, which in her distraction had stopped massaging, back on his shaft and led it up and down more forcefully. "Now where was I? Hmmmm, yes, our children of the flowers and peace and dropping out. Maybe they're trying to live Keats, I'll give them that—"

She sat upright suddenly, pulling her hand out of his crotch. "—it really shouldn't be such a difficult thing, you know, to walk around the city. To daydream. I realize that." Blurred thoughts had been gathering as he spoke. "I want to be like the others. I don't want to be different. I don't know why the carsickness comes. I hate it. It's horrible. And I realize the things I've wanted to do lately are strange, could be seen as strange . . . but they don't seem strange to me. I don't know what else to do.

"And that's the problem, you see. Nothing feels safe. The banks do, but nothing else. I don't know why." He was jerking himself off now as she spoke, grabbing at her breasts. But she was not aware of him. "I need to get to a new place. I thought maybe it was the valley, or a kind of house. If I could only get to this new place, it would all make sense."

She was so lost in thought she didn't notice him coming until he spurted his semen onto her lap. She sat a bit stunned, hazy. He hung his head, shuddering for several moments. Then he got up wordlessly and came back with a kitchen towel and tossed it to her.

"In the end it'll all be shot," he said, picking up where he had left off, as if he'd spilled some milk on her. "All the old rules won't matter. Transcendence and pleasure and unboundedness, that'll be the new society."

"But that can't be it."

". . . making love and rapping . . . " He hiked up her dress and pulled down her underpants.

"No, that's not right either. I don't want that." She felt an urgent desire to get back to something. They had been on the verge of answering all the questions. Of uncovering a transformative truth. But after wiping off the semen, the room overtook her again, the alien objects and the assault of words and nudity. As his fingers worked between her legs, she had no energy to fight, against the questions, the incongruities. "Yes, maybe you're right, maybe . . ."

"You're lovely," he whispered.

"No, not that. Everyone says that. Talk about the fear again . . . the grinding."

Later she could not remember when they had switched to wine or moved to the bedroom. She could not recall any more of what they said, except that she'd kept wanting to get back to the earlier thing, the real conversation. She seemed to remember having his penis in her mouth. She seemed to remember his waking up in the middle of the night and whispering in her ear, "Take me with you," as he held her. But she was not sure this wasn't a dream.

Her first awareness the next morning was the searing hangover, then the throbbing foot. The wound now pulpy and sore. It took a moment of staring at the door and the white-and-black-checkered rug to piece together where she was. The university man slept with his mouth open. She listened to his breath sputter like a boy's. After several minutes of lying there, she brought her hand to his cheek. His eyes opened. He blinked at B., clearly attempting to place her, then launched into a hacking cough. Eventually he settled red-faced into the pillow.

"Well, hello," he said. His voice was tired, neutral.

He rubbed his eyes with the heels of his palms. "Well. We got a little sidetracked from your medical care. We need to put that gauze on your foot. We'll fix you up and get you back on the road."

"I'm not in any hurry. I can stay awhile." She thought she might tell him about the checks. Maybe he could help her be done with them.

"Well, no, you can't stay." He spoke to the ceiling, his voice still neutral. "I'm married."

"I realize that," she replied. A distant sinking sensation went through her. "I thought maybe we could talk more. I like talking with you."

He did not move his eyes from the ceiling. "I have some things I need to get to. My wife is coming back soon and there are some things around the house I promised I'd work on . . . "

He went on about the house, its gutters or hot water heater or some other domestic concern. She lay rigid, understanding she would need to move quickly, to locate her dress, slip it on without zipping. But for the moment she did not want to move. A Johnny Mercer song came into her head. She waited inside

"I'm Old Fashioned" for some clarity or consolation; there was only her aching body in the bed.

"Good luck on your trip," the professor said abruptly, apparently at the end of his monologue. Then she knew she must go.

The house in the morning no longer looked quaint and comforting but disordered and stained, unwashed plates and cups on bookshelves, crumpled boxer shorts on the floor, discolorations in the rug. The charcoal nudes unmistakably thrusting, hostile. She found her heels near the couch. The African mask mocking her with its foreign, turned-up mouth and slitted eyes.

She ran through the campus, her foot a violent sting. The Mustang was not where she thought it was. She limped down the first street and then the next, identical in its dumpiness, and began to panic—had the car been stolen, towed? Why did it all look the same?—until she found the car dirty and untouched on the first street and wondered how she had missed it. She sat hunched at the wheel. The carsickness was a single crushing shot through the hangover and wounded foot.

She waited in the Mustang for the bank to open. A white banner draped across the top of the doors offering free toasters to new students. There was a foul smell in the car from the uneaten tacos but she did not want to handle them before going in, so she sat in the heat with the odor. She glanced at herself in the rearview mirror, catching the glint of the diamond brooch in the narrow rectangle, the mussed hair and dried makeup.

There was only one teller at the counter. A man.

Disappointment passed through her. She walked through the velvet ropes to wait her turn although there were no other customers. The male teller had his head down, arranging some papers. He made her wait several more minutes.

"Next, please."

"Hello. I'd like to make this check out to cash."

He peered at the check. "Are you visiting, ma'am?"

"Yes. My cousin."

He did not smile at her. He was young, but his brown hair was thinning at the top. His face was narrow and white, his lips pale, like two aged scars in his face.

"It's so hot over here," she said, trying to make small talk. "I didn't realize. The city is so cold in the summer."

He nodded and did not move to open his cash drawer or ask what bill denominations she preferred. She did not like the purple pattern of his tie. He studied the check again. "If you'll excuse me for a moment."

As he walked away, toward a row of desks at the back, and as he stopped to speak with another man, older and gray-haired, B. felt suddenly as if she had handed over her small child to a stranger. The male teller and the older man talked in low tones, the older man studying the check now; both looked over at B. She had an urge to run around the counter and snatch back her small child.

"Good morning, miss," the older man was saying as he approached her, "there seems to be a question on the account—"

"I just realized, I'm late. I'll have to come back." She slid the ostrich-skin purse onto her wrist and backed slowly and casually away. She walked with the same casualness out the door. Eleven steps. Outside the sun struck her, harsh and bright. She opened the Mustang door, sat down in the seat, keyed the ignition and sped out of the parking lot in one fluid motion.

20.

SHE DID NOT GO INTO her motel room, just sat by the pool in the scalding sun. She cried, watching the oiled rainbow swirls in the water. A housekeeper asked if she needed the manager; she shook her head. Her shoulders and scalp burned and her feet puckered to numbness.

The tears were not for the university man, she knew. They came from an alien, frightening place. When she finished, she dragged herself to her room, exhausted and cotton-mouthed as if coming through a desert. She lay on the bed and tried to think what she could do without the banks. What could she do without the banks? She clutched the bed, hearing the Johnny Mercer song until she fell asleep.

21.

SHE DID NOT CALL HIM from the motel. She waited, stalling, until she was back on the road. She forced herself off at a truck-weighing station. The sun was burning on the glass of the phone booth, the glare reminding her how much time there was to kill before lunch.

"Hello," she said.

"Well," Daughtry said. "Didn't expect a call from you."

The concrete sidewalk radiated more heat into the glass. Sweat gathered at the base of B.'s back, between her legs.

She tried again to remember his first name. It would not come to her.

"How are you?"

"You sound like shit," Daughtry said.

She nodded, forgetting he couldn't see her.

"How's your granny?" he asked.

"Better. Thank you."

"Bullshit."

She looked down and noted the faintest film of semen still on her dress. She began scratching it off.

"It doesn't matter," Daughtry said. "I didn't mean it. Truth is I've missed you."

"Me too," she lied. "Look, I need your help. I need more checks." She tried to keep the desperation out of her voice.

She heard him light a cigarette, the paper crumpling as he sucked. "And here I thought you just missed me."

The cigarette paper crinkling and exhales went on for several seconds before he spoke again.

"What happened to the other checks?"

"I lost them."

He laughed. "Now I know you're full of shit. What is it, drugs? You got an uncle in gambling trouble?"

She didn't answer.

"Because it can't be for the kicks. That would be too stupid: you don't need the money but you wanna get dirty. You wanna be bad. Right?"

"It's not for kicks," she said.

"You're a good girl. Period. Can't change that. You should be glad to be good." He exhaled. "I'd give anything to be good with you."

"I'll cut you in," she blurted out. She ignored in her mind his pained face. She visualized only the checks.

"What happened to them?" he finally said. "You kill the account?"

"I think so."

"See, now this is where I wonder what the fuck I'm doing. Giving them to you in the first place. Why I'm even thinking of continuing in this line with you, like a goddamn whipped twelve-year-old. Ditch the checks if you haven't already," he said. "Get rid of the ID."

In his tone of warning she heard only, regretfully, that she would have to abandon the false surname. She'd liked her picture beside the meaningless name.

"I've missed you," she tried.

His voice came out low and quiet. "The first time I saw you, I thought, it don't matter what you say to her because she'll never go out with you. I could have recited the goddamn Latin mass. You were like a painting behind glass, not the ones now but the old ones with queens and ladies in dresses, soft . . . It's ruined now, but I keep wanting to touch the glass."

"Daughtry."

"When are you coming back to the city?"

"I might not. I don't know."

"What the hell are you talking about? You wanna stay in the sticks?"

She was silent.

"You got no right to fuck with me," he said in the low voice again. "I believed you, about us not being so different. So I'm asking you, please, don't fuck with me."

"I get this feeling," she said finally. "I can't breathe, I'm going to be sick. Just walking around the city makes me sick."

"You should go to a doctor."

"No," she said, raising her palm to the hot glass. "You see, I'm not really sick. It's just a feeling. There's nowhere it's better. Only the banks make it better."

"You shoulda got married by now," Daughtry said. "Had some kids. That would make it better. You shouldn't be hanging out with guys like me."

She knew he was fishing for reassurance but she was too caught up in her own thoughts. "I don't know the reason," she said faintly. Her palm hurt on the hot glass, but she did not remove it. "I'm not trying to trick you. You're helping me. The checks help me."

"You're conning me. I'm gonna get conned in this deal, is all I see. Put out with the trash. Call me when you have a straight story," he said and hung up the phone.

22.

THE GROCERY STORE WAS OFF an exit. A pink rectangular building with a revolving plaster pig on top. The lot was almost empty. She sat in the Mustang, waiting to feel ready. It might not be so different from the banks, she told herself. Maybe more fun, more transporting. She could buy pints of ice cream, apples. She watched a feeble-looking man totter out with a bag in the crook of his arm. She took the checkbook from her purse and wrote "Cash" on the top one and ripped it out. Then she did not move. She wanted another bank. But the image of the thin-haired scar-lipped teller broke through this thought. She forced herself out of the Mustang.

Inside the air felt warm, even in the frozen section. She walked aimlessly up and down aisles. The walls were dirty green, the floor dishwater-colored linoleum. The aisles were crowded with boxes and cans, all of which looked the same to her. She felt as if they were pressing in on her. She decided she did not need to look like she was shopping. At the front two cashiers chatted back and forth; only one seemed to be working. B. waited behind an elderly woman with a basket of tuna cans and celery. The working cashier looked no older than twenty, ratted hair swirled on top of her head and dyed a harsh yellow that made her skin too pink. The other looked possibly B.'s age, her jawline beginning to slide into her neck a bit. She had short hair and thick black eyeliner that came out to triangles at the corners of her eyes.

"I don't care what he said," the short-haired one was saying, her arms crossed on the divider next to the register. "He's got no job, he's gonna get snagged by the army and probably killed. How's he providing when you're laid up?"

"He's working the harvest at Michaelson's. And I know what you're thinking." The bowl of harsh yellow hair quivered on the younger one as she rang up items. "But he's done with all that. He's not into that anymore."

The older cashier shook her head, clucking her tongue.

"We went swimming in the river last week," the younger one said. "You know what's funny? I haven't been in the river since I was a kid."

"But what's he like *out* of the river is the thing," the black-triangle-eyeliner woman said. "Still no job, still no future. Which means no future for you, get it?"

When B.'s turn came at the register, she asked about cashing the check.

"What? I can't hear you."

"Please, I need to cash this." She held up the paper.

"Charlie!" the yellow-haired girl yelled.

A fat man emerged from an aisle, clipboard in his right hand, looking preoccupied.

"ID?" he asked B.

"Oh." B. remembered to widen her eyes, bite her lip. "It's in my other purse. I'm sorry about that." She brought her hand to the diamond brooch, stroked her shoulder with her finger. The manager scanned her with his irritated face, nodded his head and then turned the check over on the clipboard and wrote on the back. "Don't forget it next time," he said tiredly. B. nodded.

The yellow-haired cashier rang open the drawer. "It was so nice at the river, Dee," she said, not even looking as she counted out the fifty dollars to B. "Why couldn't it be like that all the time? How d'you know it wouldn't?"

The bills were ragged, torn fives and tens, soft and old. B. forced herself not to pull her hand back.

"It never stays like at the river, honey."

B. was out in the blinding sun with the fistful of bills.

The cashier's horrible hair quivered in her mind, the other's black triangles, and the carsickness rose into her throat. None of the calm of the banks. She braced against the door of the Mustang. She wanted to lay her spinning head on the roof but the metal was blistering. The cool expansive feeling must come. She waited. A woman wheeled out a heaping cart with a red-mouthed toddler in the front kicking and screaming over the bar. The woman spoke to him in a robotically soothing voice. Her hair looked limp and dull in the sun, her face drawn.

All the women in the valley looked tired, B. thought.

The carsickness surged. The cool expansive feeling did not come.

The toddler's stained mouth shrieked. The woman tossed the bags into the back of the station wagon, still speaking as if by rote. B. held her stomach and steadied herself against the Mustang. Without thinking, she walked toward the woman as the last bag went in, the toddler shrieking almost in her ear. The woman ignored B. standing there. She slammed the rear door and pulled the child out of the cart, onto her hip. "I have some extra money," B. blurted out. The woman gave no signal that she had heard B. She put the boy in the front seat and slammed the door, walked stone-faced back to the driver's side. The boy's attention turned to B. and his wailing stopped, as if a television had been switched on. The woman sat still in the driver's seat for a moment. "I have a husband," she said through the window. "I ain't no charity case, so whatever born-again Jehovah's Witness racket this is, go fuck yourself." Then she started the engine, the toddler still fixed on B. as if she'd exploded or dropped off a cliff in a cartoon. They peeled out of the parking lot and B. stood in the exhaust.

This time she did not feel any urge to cry. Like an automaton she got into the car. She drove with the dirty grocery store bills in her right hand. Daughtry was in her thoughts somewhere, chiding. Her skull spun; she felt the whiteness on the inside of her jaw from clenching.

On the road back to the freeway, she passed a group of Chinese men huddled in a vacant lot in the thin shade of a pepper tree, smoking on their haunches. She stopped the Mustang. She walked over to them and threw down the crumpled grocery store bills. The men kept smoking, staring without speaking. Back in the car, she realized that she would rather at that moment be any one of them, with their strange eyes and stained teeth and dirty undershirts.

When she was back on the freeway, she lifted her hands off the wheel and closed her eyes. Eventually she opened them again. She lowered her hands back down but did not let her foot up off the gas.

23.

THE PLUM TREES WERE ENDLESS dark masses blotting the pale blue sky. She followed the gray trunks. She focused on getting to the end of each field, each orchard. One to the next, forward motion.

The girl from Sambo's was not even standing when she came upon her, but sitting on her knapsack, her bare brown legs in the cutoffs splayed in front of her. She wore the same white peasant blouse, now with a brown suede vest over, her feet shoeless. When B. stopped the car, the girl did not look surprised or grateful, just stood up and bent into the open window.

"You going to Reno?"

B. shook her head.

"Me either."

The girl climbed in without another word or a second look

at B., settling her knapsack on the floor. She unbuttoned the suede vest and stuffed it inside, rummaged for her cigarettes and lit one.

B. could see the girl's breasts clearly through the peasant blouse. She pulled the car back on the road. The girl smoked and stared out the window, as if there was nothing inside the car to hold her attention.

"I'm going to San Francisco," she finally said on one of her exhales. "But not yet. My old man is there. But I don't need that scene right now." A half dozen silver bracelets clinked at her wrist as she raised and lowered the cigarette.

"I used to live there," B. said. "I don't think I'm going back."

The girl did not seem to hear her. They passed an empty fruit stand, the bright red-lettered sign for CORN & APRICOTS TODAY giving the impression that someone might show up any minute. Hot grainy air blew around the car, whipping the girl's long hair.

The girl held the cigarette between her lips and knotted the hair behind her. "We were camping for a while at the beach. My parents never took us to the ocean. Just pools. Chlorine and water wings and all that noise. Anyway, I told him he could leave for San Fran if he wanted, I was staying. He left."

B. could not make sense of any part of this statement. "Where are you from?" she asked.

"Fontana. Wasteland of America." General images of the southern half of the state rolled through B.'s mind, orange

groves and salmon-colored houses and women in white sun-
glasses. B. saw in her peripheral vision the glint of blonde hair
all over the girl's legs. Her fingernails were grimed black. They
drove through an alfalfa field (she knew from the scattering but-
terflies), and past a small house with two date palms in front and
a dead olive tree in back. B. wondered whether she'd already
driven down this road.

"It's a drag because he'll miss me." The girl drew a finger back
and forth across her chapped lips. "Yeah, it'll be a real downer for
him. But like I said, I have my own scene—see things, do things."

The nausea thrummed through B. She tried to concentrate
on what was happening inside the Mustang, on how the girl had
come to be beside her, but she was having trouble processing all
of it, the hair, the breasts, the dirt.

"What have you seen?" she said carefully through the thrumming.

"Lots of stuff. I saw my first real Indian the other day. I mean
I've seen them hustling at concerts, but this one was real. He
drove a bus and wore a funky necklace of feathers and beads
with his uniform, and his hair was down his back. His nose was
big. He looked angry.

"And I saw the governor's mansion. Jed and those groupies
would think it's too straight. But if people visit, it's for a reason."

B. tried and failed to picture the girl shuffling behind a velvet
rope next to families and silver-haired retirees. It was at this
moment she realized the girl had no recollection of her.

"What have you seen?" the girl asked indifferently.

B. flushed. "I saw the Sutter Buttes. They're mountains in the middle of the valley, not connected to anything, you see. It makes them interesting."

The girl tilted her head back against the seat, eyes on the window.

"I've never been picked up by a woman before."

"I don't mind," was all B. could think of to say.

"You should go to the governor's mansion," the girl said without enthusiasm.

They drove past another alfalfa field. A slinky metal irrigation machine wheeled through it but there was no one to see; a machine somewhere to make it run. B. understood this about the valley now.

The girl had already fallen asleep, snoring lightly. B. kneaded her temple. The thrum was across the backside of her eyes, down the base of her neck. A be-in type in her car now, a "crazy," a "stinko," the secretaries called them, and yet she seemed to B. only like a dirty, pitiable child. B. told herself that she must make a plan. To get back to the banks, yes, but then for after. This was what she must do. Because even if she got back to the banks, she had the hazy understanding that they would only be available to her for a limited time. B. recalled on the wrist of the first pretty teller a charm bracelet with gold miniatures of the Eiffel Tower and the London Bridge (and a four-leaf clover and a heart with an arrow through it and a diamond chip). Well B. could go abroad too, couldn't she? She could go to Paris and Rome.

But she saw quaint woven straw chairs and mansard roofs and sensed that this kind of plan was too similar to what she'd already done, coming west.

The thrumming went on.

All at once the heat returned to her again, the air flattening. A suffocation that mixed with the girl and the non-plan and the thrumming. There was no breathing. She pulled over. She got out and began walking blindly into a field. It was not until she saw a flash of red and smelled the sharp stickiness of the vines that she realized she was back in one of the tomato fields. Going on and on, helter-skelter, shadeless. But she had to move. The bone-colored heels caught in the crumbled dirt. Her face felt swollen. She wondered suddenly what she looked like to the girl. She reached into the purse for her compact. In the sunlight, her skin was pink and glazed, her throat beginning to sag, the skin draping slightly at her chin. Blackheads were visible in her pores, broken capillaries around her nose. She had, until recently, applied a facial mask every week to slough off old skin and expose new, as her mother had taught her.

She should try to find a facial mask in the valley.

The sound of splattering turned her around. The girl was squatted beside the Mustang, peeing in the dirt.

"I could have driven you somewhere," B. said confusedly,

stumbling back toward the car. "We could have stopped for you to . . . urinate."

"I didn't want to *urinate* on your seat." The girl stood up and buttoned her cutoffs and made no move to get back in the car. "You wanna get high?" She took a small cigarette from behind her ear. B. shook her head. "Suit yourself, it's good. Jamaican." The girl walked past her into the field, her skin brown and firm in the sun. She took long drags on the joint and pulled tomatoes from the ground, tossing them as far as she could.

Now B. could not stand the tomato fields one minute longer. "We should get going," she called.

The girl had picked a yellow tomato and was trying to look through it. "Going where?" she asked.

B.'s head throbbed, her scalp burned. "Well, I just stopped for a second. I'd rather keep moving."

The girl shrugged. "I'm hungry," she said.

"You'll have to put on some shoes if we stop."

"I have shoes."

Each square of land they passed was bleached in the heat and smog and against the washed-out sky. B. felt as if she'd always been in the valley. Daughtry's voice came into her head. Throw the checks out. They'll be looking for you. She shook it off. She concentrated on the bleached squares while the girl stared out the window. Finally they came on a sign for a roadside bar and restaurant. OPEN ALL DAY.

The front and back doors of the bar-restaurant were open,

a sunlit tunnel into darkness. Fans on the ceiling spun but did not create any breeze. B. was relieved there were no other customers. She did not want to be seen with the girl. A man stacking glasses behind the counter took their orders and they sat down.

The girl ate her hamburger with a meticulousness that surprised B., French fries first, then the hamburger patty, then the pickle, placing the other trimmings inside the bun and closing it firmly. B. picked at her spaghetti. It had seemed the safest choice for the throbbing and spinning and heat but the noodles coagulated in a thick cloying sauce.

"What do you think you'll do, in San Francisco?" she asked the girl.

The girl had been spearing the hamburger bun with her fork. "I don't know. Hang out."

"You don't really have a plan."

The girl looked up from her stabbing and B. thought she might jab the fork at her but her face was expressionless. "Are we going soon?" she said. She got up and walked toward the jukebox.

B. stroked the ostrich-skin purse. The girl, she knew, would not offer any money. B. felt unwilling again to part with the bank bills. In the deep of her mind, Daughtry was warning her in his low bitter voice.

"It's so silly of me," she said to the man behind the bar. "I forgot my cash in my other purse. Do you take checks?"

The man ran his eyes over her. "You from Sacramento?" he asked.

"I'm on a trip with my daughter, to Reno." She paused and softened her voice. "We're going to meet my husband. He's on business there. He won't be surprised to hear I brought the wrong purse." She handed him the check. "There's extra for the tip, of course."

The man looked at her. "I don't know this bank, ma'am."

"Oh, it's in the city. I can endorse it in front of you here." She opened the purse, fumbled inside. "Well, I thought I had . . . Do you have a pen?" She smoothed her hair back, realizing she could not remember the last time she'd brushed it.

He reached next to the register and handed her a pen.

"I'll just take down your driver's license number," he said.

"Yes, of course." She rummaged the open purse again and dropped her shoulders, pretending exasperation. "Well, of all things. My license is in my other purse as well. Harold will think I'm hilarious."

"I need some kind of identification, ma'am."

"You could use my license plate."

She was reading a script in her mind, without examining any of the lines. Behind the bar, a black-and-white pinup photo from the 1940s was glossy and signed. A girl in a one-piece, curls on top of her head, long legs in seamed-stockings and platform heels, peeping over her shoulder. B. could not quite make out the inscription. BE LIGHT! ME TONIGHT! (TAKE

FLIGHT?) On the check she wrote out an amount larger than the bill.

"Ma'am?"

"I can write the license number down for you," B. heard herself saying next. She clutched the pen, beginning to write.

"No, I'll get it myself. That's yours over there?" The man gestured through the open door to the Mustang.

He stepped outside with his pad. B. stood in the doorway. The girl was busy examining the jukebox as if it were a riddle from a distant time. B. watched the man walk around the car, tilting his head. He went around the back and wrote on his pad. He came back inside and slipped the check into the register and counted out, minus the commission and tip, her change.

He looked B. in the eye. "I sure hope you're not scamming me. I'd hate to send two pretty ladies to jail."

Be light! Take flight!

"I don't know what you mean."

In the bathroom before they left, she tried to stick her finger down her throat. She only gagged. She knew not to expect the cool expansive feeling. But the throbbing seemed worse now. A new feeling of dread came over her, a feeling that she was heading the wrong way, that she should have turned or stopped somewhere earlier. Her body felt suddenly exhausted. The girl had gone outside, kicking at the dust of the parking lot, the loose thin leather that barely held together her sandals and her feet covered in dirt.

"I can't drive any more today," B. said in the car. "I think we should stop at a motel."

The girl looked straight at B. for the first time. "I don't do anything like that, okay?" The girl's eyes were brown and tired.

"No. I meant . . . it's too hot. I just want to rest. I'd rather drive in the morning."

The eyes took this in. "If you're paying."

B. stopped at the next roadside motel and got them a room with two double beds. Dark blue bedspreads with giant purple and red flowers. The girl went into the bathroom. B. heard the shower turn on. While she could she went back to the car and hid the checkbook in the glove compartment and the money under the seat. Then she lay back on one of the beds. The rough texture of the nylon threads scratched her legs but she did not move or turn down the comforter. There seemed to be glitter in the ceiling. She stared at the glitter and went through in her mind all the actions she could take right at that moment: get up, rip up the checks, change clothes, get into the car, go back to the city. She lay there, immobile. The dizziness held steady. The shower ran for a while and she realized she herself had not bathed in days. After the girl finished, she would shower. They would sleep. She would have coffee and a real breakfast in the morning and be able to drive for hours. Drive farther away. Perhaps she could find other quiet places, not like the super- market or the bar. Department stores, maybe. But she would have to go into cities for that. She sat up and saw herself in the mirror across from the bed. She was sunburned, thin. Her dark roots were showing. Her cuticles dirty and her knuckle with a large cut, she could not remember how. She could start there: bathe, clean her fingernails. And yet she did not want to move, did not have the energy to scrub anything. Maybe it was better to let all these thoughts go. Maybe a plan would come to her that way, descend from somewhere. She held the vague recognition that someone might be after her now. The police. The people to whom the checks belonged. Daughtry. But the considerations were shadowy, faint, like a bell tolling in the distance.

When the girl emerged from the bathroom she was wearing a long T-shirt, through which her nipples showed, wet hair hanging down to her ribs. B. saw clearly the dark circles under her eyes, beneath the tan.

"I usually watch TV."

"Okay," B. said.

The girl pushed the button on the box and sat on the other bed. A variety show came on and a series of ladies in black shorts with cummerbunds and tuxedo jackets spun canes and tipped their top hats. They did not sing, but moved in perfect mute unison, one woman with a big white smile, false eyelashes and a bow tie. When they finished a bald man came on and made jokes to a recorded laugh track.

"Aren't you going to shower?" the girl asked.

"I just want to rest first." B. lay back against her pillow. The skin over her body was tight from the sun and heat. Had she brought any body cream? The variety show ended and next they watched a talk show, a man in a corduroy suit in an armchair across from an actress in another armchair. The woman wore a minidress with a large bow, a pixie haircut and exaggerated eyelashes, making her look like a Pierrot. The host made jokes about the actress's last film role; the actress smiled stiffly. The girl sat smoking and laughing at the jokes.

"Where are we?" B. asked.

"I dunno. Somewhere near Marysville."

After a while, B. said, "Does it help, traveling around?"

"Help what?"

"I thought maybe you left for some reason. To get away from something."

"From dying of boredom," the girl said. "Cement plant, pinochle club on Saturday nights, Blue Hawaiians before dinner." Her wet hair made mottled, transparent spots in her shirt. She inhaled the cigarette deeply, let all the smoke out before she spoke again.

"When Jed had enough money, we split. I called my mom from Fresno. She cried. Worrying is her thing. Worrying and cleaning. She's never been farther than L.A. for Christ's sake."

The actress on the talk show was now laughing and flirting, but still stiffly, making the Pierrot effect more marked. Her lips moved in a quiet white-pink murmur. When the talk show host asked about her love life she put her fingers in front of her mouth.

"I was sick in the city, that's why I left," B. said. "I think I was dying." It seemed true. "Do your parents know where you are now?" she asked.

The girl ignored the question. "Where are you going, anyway?" she asked.

"I don't know. Around the valley."

The girl continued to smoke and watch the show, genuinely pulled in it seemed. The comedian came back on and continued his shtick. The girl laughed again at his jokes.

"It was a kind of nausea, the reason I left the city," B. went on. "I don't suppose you've ever felt that way?"

"I puked as a kid."

"But have you ever felt a nausea that wasn't . . . I mean, did you ever feel carsick when you weren't really?"

The girl rose and rooted through the knapsack until she pulled out the crumpled magazine from the Sambo's floor and flopped back on the bed. "I don't get carsick," she said.

The girl's dirty fingernails, not clean even after the shower, closed around the crumpled white veil. The comedian finished and a woman brought on a short gray dog that flipped backward on command.

B. suddenly shivered. "The air-conditioning's too high," she said aloud. She got up and flicked the knob down.

After that she went into the bathroom, but the idea of

showering exhausted her. She swiped her armpits with a wash-cloth, splashed her face and went back to the bed, listening to the girl laugh to the laugh track on television.

———————•———————

In Boston she had wanted to make friends with another woman. She thought perhaps her mother was right, it might help her to be more gay and light, it might help with the car-sickness, and so she'd tried with Louise.

Louise was an old college dorm mate who lived in New York. When B. phoned her she seemed very eager to meet. "I'll drive up today." They met at a restaurant near B.'s apartment and Louise talked nonstop from the moment of their first martini.

"I volunteered for a while, you know, MoMA. One of the other girls was young, a coed. She would read these awful poems that went on and on and didn't rhyme." Louise sighed. "She wore blue jeans all the time and smoked grass and I thought it was really sort of disgusting, but she liked me, you see. Maybe subconsciously she had some kind of effect, an influence of some kind."

B. did not know what to do with this flood of words from another woman but it did not matter because Louise asked her nothing, just went on talking about New York and drinking more martinis. At some point her face turned slack with alcohol.

"Anyhow, I had this day—we have a horrible little flat in the

Thirties but Ed is working his way up in the firm, you know, we'll have a whole floor on the Upper East soon—well, I was trying to cook a roast in that silly little kitchen with no counter space and so I used our little table to chop the vegetables and then I was on the floor with the roasting pan because there was nowhere else to put it. I was trying to arrange all the trimmings and he came home and found me and laughed at me. He thought it was unbelievably funny somehow, me on the floor. And I don't know what made me so mad . . . I don't know what I was thinking . . . I bit him. I grabbed his arm and bit him! Have you ever heard of such a juvenile thing? And he laughed at that too. He thought I was being . . . romantic." Louise's eyes were large in the slack face as she spoke. "But I felt like biting his other arm, really gnawing his skin, and we made love right there on the kitchen floor—I can't believe I'm telling you this—and that part was fine. But he fell asleep afterward, there on the floor, and he was snoring, and of course, yes, he works those long hours, but there I was with the roast uncooked and him snoring. And I walked out. I didn't even bring my coat, you know. Already fall, but I wasn't thinking—not even my coat! I kept walking until my teeth chattered. I didn't even have money for a hotel, so I stayed with a friend, told her Ed was out of town on business and I was too scared to stay in the apartment alone, and she laughed at me too—everyone considered me just *hilarious* that day—and that night I went back and told him I was leaving him. And the funny part is I still don't know why.

"My family doesn't know yet. Well, no one really knows. When you called, I took that as a sign! I could move up here near you. A new city, fresh start. We could go out together."

"I don't go out much."

"Well, we could start, you know. We could have cocktail parties and potlucks and things."

"Maybe you should go back to Ed," was all B. could think of to say.

Louise's slack face shook. "I didn't think you'd say that. I thought you of all people would say something else."

B. tried then to tell Louise about the carsickness. But the other woman stiffened. "Well that's quite strange," she said coldly. "You should see a doctor." B. told her she had and it hadn't helped, and after that Louise grew quiet and said she was going to vomit from the martinis and B. took her home.

She passed out on B.'s couch. In the morning, Louise's black makeup flaked under her eyes and her cheeks were rutted from the couch. She made a fuss about an early appointment and spilled her coffee in her rush to leave. After that the rug was stained and the carsickness was worse and B. decided to try San Francisco.

———————•———————

SHE WOKE UP SOMETIME AFTER midnight. The television was blaring a rainbow screen. She switched it off. The girl snored lightly, mouth open, arms flung out across the bed and hair splashed across the pillow, face calm and untroubled.

B. went into the bathroom for her travel bag—she could at least comb her hair. But when she opened the bag she found her nightgown folded neatly on top. How many days now had she slept in the dresses? She took out the nightgown and held it up before her, the filmy length pleating onto the floor. Then she removed the top of the back of the toilet, lifted the nightgown by one finger, and sank it into the water. It billowed like a last gasp. She forced it under and replaced the lid.

She walked back into the bedroom and watched the sleeping girl. B. was closer to the girl's mother's age, she realized. The girl's mother having undoubtedly worn the kid gloves, danced with the Brylcreemed boys, perhaps received her own vanity set. The realization made B. sad and weary. The girl's knapsack was next to the bed. B. opened it. The notebook was on top. She held it up to her face but she could not make out the words in the dark. The girl moved. B. put the notebook back in the knapsack and crept into bed.

24.

THEY SLEPT IN THE WARM room until noon. The bill when they checked out was too much to use just the roadhouse money. B. excused herself to the car for a moment and reached under the seat. When the clerk counted out her change, she stared at the dirty worn bills in place of the beautiful crisp one. She shoved them in the ostrich-skin purse. Outside, the carsickness was in full bloom. Her temples pounding and jaw clenched in the searing parking lot with dead grass in its cracks. In the rear-view mirror, she noted the sallow flecks in the whites of her eyes, the lines in her forehead.

They stopped for gas. B. hooked one of the rusty pumps into the gas tank and leaned against the car. Her gaze landed passively around her. On her legs, sunburned and growing hair. On the filthy bone-colored heels. On the back of the girl's head, the white part in the two braids and the blonde down against the brown neck. Next to the gas station a dun-colored eucalyptus break stood motionless in the heat. B. watched it, waiting for movement. She decided she could make her plan later. She could drive with the girl for now. Why not.

When the tank was full she went inside and returned with coffees and two packages of doughnuts.

"I don't eat that," the girl said.

"Oh." B. hesitated, then slid both packages under the seat. "The guy inside said there's a gold rush park just down the highway."

The girl did not look up. "We studied it in school." She was flipping again through the torn *LIFE* magazine. B. sipped her coffee, hiking up her dress to rest the paper cup between her legs. She liked the idea of her legs splayed like the girl's. But she did not want to see the magazine again, the magazine agitated her. She started the engine and drove past the eucalyptus break, where no branch had moved.

"Which direction should we go?" B. asked.

"I don't care," said the girl. "Not Sacramento."

B. took a road north. The girl lit a cigarette. The smoke and the musky scent and the half-nakedness felt more normal in the car now. Today, the girl wore only the suede vest, without a bra, and the jean cutoffs. Long gray feathers were braided into her hair on each side of her head. She fiddled with the radio until a rock-and-roll station flickered in and out. A man was singing low to an accompaniment of calliope bells. B. tried to open her mind to the bells, to the man's slithering tones. But the odd notes and exhortations seemed to highlight the dirt and dead insects on the windshield, the trash on the road.

"Maybe I should head to San Francisco," the girl said. "Jed is probably sick of them by now, waiting for me. He told me we're soul mates from another life. Like a cosmic link. Like I'm his Cleopatra, his old lady from another time." B. was sure Jed was no Anthony but held her tongue. "So those dingbats can ball him all they want. For now." The girl put her feet up on the dashboard and picked at some open skin on her knee.

"Maybe you should go," B. said.

The girl turned to the window. "Maybe."

They drove through an eerie stretch of wooden stakes high in the ground. Unnaturally bright green vines climbing up the brown wood. B. finally understood they were hops. She had the sensation from the stakes that she and the girl were filing through enemy lines, row by row bellying to the other side.

She could feel the girl staring at her now. "You're pretty," the girl observed in her impassive tone. "Like a movie star."

B. fingered the diamond brooch. "Thank you."

"I'd rather look like *something*," the girl went on. "Like Janis Joplin."

"You don't seem like a drifter," she added.

"I'm not drifting. I'm visiting. I might stay." B.'s mind folded up the defeats of the realtor, the university man, the grocery store in her mind. She made herself see the valley as a long golden plane and herself golden in it. She deliberately did not think of the checks or the banks.

"Driving, drifting, whatever . . . You still don't seem the type."

The golden image vanished. "What about you?" B. said testily. "You're drifting."

"But I'm young," the girl concluded in her flat tone.

The inside of B.'s head lurched.

"I haven't decided my plans yet," B. said.

"This country has it all wrong," the girl said. "I'm going to Spain. Andalusia."

"Spain is ruled by a dictator. It's authoritarian."

"And then to Morocco. India, China, Istanbul, you get it? Forget this apple pie bullshit."

"The Chinese are Communists," B. said faintly.

The girl brought her feet up on the dashboard, picking at the calluses on her toes. She whistled "Yankee Doodle Dandy" through her teeth as she pulled at small springy strips of dead skin.

B. realized then that a black car had been in the rearview for some time. A kind of sedan.

The girl closed her eyes and scratched her legs absentmindedly.

B. had not seen any other black sedans in the valley.

The girl was raking her nails up and down, eyes still closed, and B. saw then the scabs like raspberries across her skin.

"That's poison oak," B. said. "You need ointment."

"Ointment," the girl repeated.

She opened her eyes and looked irritatedly at B. "I left my mother in Fontana."

"I'm just telling you, that's poison oak. We should find a druggist."

The girl sat up and examined her shins. She sucked at her teeth. "When the fuck did that happen?"

"You don't wear any stockings."

"Are you kidding me?"

B. glanced back at the black sedan. It was several lengths behind them. She continued on the two-lane highway. She would try to avoid the freeways now, she decided. At the first intersection the gas station attendant with his large green-peaked pimples pointed them east for a pharmacy. B. drove and when she realized the black sedan was no longer behind them, she felt no relief.

They reached the town and the pharmacy and B. stepped out of the car, smoothing her dress out of habit, the wrinkles now deep in the fabric. The girl crossed her arms, slouching in her seat.

"I don't like doctors."

"It's not a doctor, don't be silly. It's just poison oak. He'll give you some medicine."

"What do you care?"

"You can't walk around with poison oak."

B. went inside, the girl following reluctantly. It was an old pharmacy with wooden counters and hundreds of drawers, a dusty film in the air blown around by table fans. B. approached the short bald man behind the counter. "We need something for poison oak, please. Do you have any calamine lotion?"

"I don't serve those types."

"Excuse me?"

He flicked his chin at the girl. "No shirt, no service. We're not over the bridge here."

"I'm paying," B. said.

He scrutinized B. for a moment. "Alright. But I don't want her in my store."

The girl was revolving a rack of support hose in the corner. The firm white sides of her breasts visible through the vest. B. whispered to her that it might be better if she waited outside, and the girl leered at the pharmacist. "Fucking pig," she said but walked out.

The man watched the door after the girl was gone. B. shoved some roadhouse money onto the counter and took the calamine lotion and cotton balls.

"Asshole bourgeois capitalist pig." The girl spat at the sidewalk.

B. did not think the girl knew what the words meant.

"Apple pie bullshit."

B. handed the girl the bottle and bag. The girl stood with them, unmoving.

"What's wrong?"

"I don't know how to do it."

"You've never put on calamine lotion? For a mosquito bite?"

"I dunno."

The girl looked at her expressionlessly. The druggist was right to be wary of such a foreign, feckless creature, B. thought. B. pulled a cotton ball out of the bag and kneeled to the girl's legs. Over each red patch she dabbed the milk and blew gently. "Just let it dry. It will help the itching. If you scratch, you'll spread it."

The girl stared down at her plastered legs.

They walked to the car in silence and the girl slouched in her seat, the white-splotched shins up against her. B. felt an unexpected lift. As if something had passed between them, small but important. Her head felt momentarily still, her body free from nausea.

"I can drive, you know," the girl said. "If you want a break."

"I like to drive."

The girl began chattering, as if she'd felt the lift too. "Jed wants to get a motorcycle, to ride around Spain . . . I'm gonna learn the guitar and how to sing. We'll ride around and earn bread playing on the streets, you know, and we'll see the country—see, go, see."

B. was trying to get inside the statements now. "But where will you stay?"

"We'll bring a tent," the girl said. "We'll live like gypsies. Be in nature and be with the people."

B. pictured the girl in a bright flamenco dress with the tiers of ruffles, a large flower in her hair. She felt a pang of envy. But it was ridiculous, wasn't it? For anyone to live that way.

"A chick I met near Fresno lived on the land with her old man. They were on a real reservation, you know, camped with the Indians. The Indians just dug what these two were getting at, they didn't even charge them. Anyway, the chick learned all kinds of prayers and dances. She taught me some." The girl ran her fingers over the braids. Her eyes narrowed as if she was deep in thought. "I think we should do one of the Indian prayers."

B. laughed. Then she saw the girl was serious.

"I thought you'd be hip to it. Being out on the road and all," the girl said.

Blood rose to B.'s cheeks. "Well, I guess so." She did not believe the girl knew a true Indian prayer. "I guess it couldn't hurt."

The girl smiled for the first time since B. had picked her up. "Pull over here," the girl directed.

They were next to a pear orchard. The trees were larger than in the other orchards and B. was secretly relieved they'd be hidden at least. The girl disappeared into one of the rows. B. followed. Halfway in, the girl picked up a stick and started carving a large circle in the dirt. "Take your shoes off," she commanded. B. removed the bone-colored heels. She did not know why she was following along.

With the same stick, the girl began drawing a sun and a moon inside the circle, very seriously, standing back at points to check her work. She added stars. The dirt was grainy between B.'s toes; she forgot the still-open cut. The pears gave off no scent, only the smell of dirt and leaves. When the girl finished the drawings, she began to orbit the circle. She put her palms up and out and began: "Dear moon, we are your children. Show us the way. Dear sun, we are your children. Show us the way." The girl's voice was loud and solemn; B. suppressed another urge to laugh. "Mother Earth, we are far away from you, we are lost. Show us the way. Show us in the stars. Sun and moon, we give ourselves to you, show us the way." The girl began to ululate. "Heya heya heya!" She sped up and began to spin and hop around the circle. The movements fascinated B.; she had not imagined the girl to have any energy at all. "Heya heya heya! Oh! . . .We don't give to the government man or the business man or the police man . . . Heya heya heya! We don't give them a goddamn thing . . . Oh! Heya heya heya! We give to the people, the people, the people." Dancing and moaning, the girl grabbed B.'s hand and pulled her along. "We give ourselves to the sun and the moon and the earth and the stars cuz we need your protection, man! We need you to show us the way! We're ready to take back the way!" B. felt ridiculous, going around in the circle, until the girl released her abruptly and she was left to watch her twirling fast in the center of the circle, arms wide, braids whipping out, utterly free.

Are you funny about women, is that it? Don't you want to be normal? Her mother's voice sharp and panicked into the phone. And B. had wanted to ask her, plead with her, "Is that all there is? Isn't there anything else?" But she'd told her mother every-thing would be fine.

B. watched the girl chanting and dancing around her. Then she stepped into the circle. She turned around slowly. Slowly, slowly the pear trees went by. The carsickness felt remote; her body empty. She began to sob.

The girl stopped. She stared with the same blank stare from Sambo's. Without a word, she turned and walked through the dirt drawings back to the Mustang. After a few moments B. fol-lowed.

They did not speak of the Indian prayer again.

THEIR MOTEL ROOM THAT NIGHT had a single queen bed with lumpy mattress, dripping faucet, cracked plaster walls. The girl fell asleep immediately while B. lay next to her aware of every breath, of the heat radiating off her brown arms and legs. She tried to count the cracks in the ceiling. The carsickness still remote; the banks abstract and unsubstantial in her thoughts.

She took the girl's hand and held it. The girl inhaling and exhaling so easily.

25.

THEY WOKE LATE AGAIN. THEY stopped for lunch and the girl devoured a meatloaf sandwich, two scoops of chocolate ice cream and an orange soda. (B. had coffee and bits of Danish.) Afterward they drove aimlessly on the small roads. It seemed easier now for B. to drive without speaking, to follow wherever the road took them, the girl's feet up on the dashboard, hot wind through the windows. (The heat itself now a welcome stupor.) The carsickness was still subdued. Maybe if she could stay this way with the girl. Maybe, she thought, something with her had cured it.

When the sun was just above the western hills, they intersected the freeway again and came on a small carnival by the side of it. The girl perked up.

"Can we stop?"

The rides were old and ramshackle. But B.'s lower back ached from driving and the girl was too excited.

"Okay," B. said.

The girl bounced in her seat until they parked. She asked B. for money and went to the entrance without waiting. It was all seedy: the half-dozen rickety rides with rusting metal and flaking paint, the faded concession stands, the operators' road-weary faces. The music *oomped-oomped* and the dingy bulbs winked. There was a whirling tilted octopus ride, bumper cars, an airplane merry-go-round for small children, a spinning column of swings. But no Ferris wheel. B. would have liked to go above the valley again; she would have liked to compare it with the buttes. The girl made her ride the bumper cars, the clanging and crashing and sparks of which B. hated, and then the octopus, which made her neck ache. When the girl insisted on riding the spinning column of swings, B. refused and she watched the girl go around, long braids and feathers sailing, face indecipherable. B. bought her a caramel apple and an ice cream cone. (The girl had not refused anything since the doughnuts.) She bought herself a bag of popcorn and they walked along the midway as the last blue in the sky blackened.

"He doesn't understand that sometimes a person just wants to see something pretty. What's wrong with that. The ocean, for example. And I thought the governor's mansion would be like Pasadena. Once on a field trip we visited a grower's mansion and I'll never forget the long curtains like silk or velvet or what-ever, all soft and shiny . . . A person just likes to see that."

Any sudden effusion was related to Jed, B. now understood. "I don't think you have to explain yourself," she said.

The girl was staring at her. "Can I wear one of your dresses?" she asked out of nowhere, chocolate ice cream in the corners of her mouth.

B. took the girl in, with her cutoffs, wearing only a lace-topped camisole and the leather choker around her neck, large turquoise in the center.

"They haven't been cleaned in a while," B. said.

The girl shrugged. "I don't care."

B. had a brief vision of the girl in her dress, on the bus through Chinatown, at the beauty salons. She held the irrational thought that perhaps the girl would understand then. Maybe then she could tell the girl about the walks and the crocus. They went back to the trunk of the Mustang, the organ music whining behind them. B. pulled the powder-blue dress from the travel bag. (She had put back on the ivory; she only wanted the ivory sheath now.) "I should really hang them up in the back," she said. "I don't know why I don't." She didn't have another pair of heels; the girl would have to wear her sandals.

"I can fix your hair and makeup," B. offered.

"Alright."

The girl changed in the backseat while B. got out her brush. When she stepped out the hard nipples were pressed against the bust of the dress. B. tried not to look. She removed the braids and feathers and brushed through the girl's hair, pulling out tangles. "Ouch. Ow!" "I can't help it, your knots are horrible." The girl's hair was too long to keep any kind of style so B. twirled it up on top of her head and arranged it like a crown with her bobby pins. Then she painted the girl's eyelids black with liner and mascaraed her long lashes and drew on the pink lipstick. B. unhooked the diamond brooch from her own chest and pinned it at the girl's collarbone. The girl eyed B. "I've never worn a diamond before." She gazed at herself in the car windows, fingering the brooch. "Like a movie star," she said. The girl's shins were still blotched white with calamine. She needed stockings, a handbag, B. thought vaguely.

They went back to the midway and walked under the winking bulbs. The girl's neck looked long with her hair up. B. watched the farmers grin but the girl did not seem to notice.

"Let's have some beer," the girl said.

B. bought two bottles and it appeared that whatever substances the girl had imbibed in her short life, she had not had much beer. She seemed immediately drunk. They sat on a wooden picnic bench and watched the crowd in the jangle of the midway and the girl babbled on about her favorite rock groups, the first time she took acid, an ice cream parlor in Fontana where her mother threw her a "goofy" six-year-old birthday party. The crowd, B. observed as the girl talked, was sunburned couples and sunburned teenagers and a few Mexicans. No other women with hitchhiking girls.

The girl kept smoothing down the wrinkles at her lap. "You must feel like a *lady* in these getups. Who wears this stuff, anyway? Hello, I'm Mrs. *Lady*."

The girl insisted on doing the swing ride again in the new outfit. But by the time she returned to the picnic bench her expression had changed back to the indifference. She slumped next to B., her head leaning to the side, a new bottle of beer somehow in her hand.

"It's too tight on me. I can't breathe."

"It fits perfectly."

The girl drank the whole beer. "You should wear my clothes now," she said.

B. did not respond. She had, in truth, wondered what they felt like, the suede and the bare legs and the leather choker. But only in passing.

"You too good for my clothes?"

"I just don't feel like changing right now."

The girl grabbed B.'s bottle out of her hand and drank that too. "You're one of those snobs," she hissed. Her eyes seemed only able to land in some middle distance beyond B. "Snobby cunt won't wear my clothes."

"It's getting late," B. said. "We should find a motel."

"Blah blah blah, you think you're too good, that's it. You think you're just driving around this shit valley for the sights or something. What *sights?* Like this?" She gestured mockingly at the midway.

"I know what you're doing," the girl went on, tossing the beer bottle in the dirt, looking slightly addled now with hair falling out of the crown, lipstick smeared. "I'm not stupid. I've seen things on the road. I want in on the action. Jed and me need the dough."

B. kept her eyes level on the midway. "I don't know what you mean."

"I mean the pile of cash under your seat."

B.'s body went oddly still, the heaving down deep where she could not feel it yet.

"Don't worry, I didn't take any." More hair fell out of its bun as she spoke, head bobbing. "How do you set up the tricks anyway? You can't just hang out on corners like in the city. Do you offer to blow the farmers at their fruit stands or something? Out in the fields?"

"You're drunk."

"One of those ladies who gets her rocks off hooking. Does your husband think you're on a reducing weekend or something?"

She yanked the girl up by the arm. The spinning instantly and violently back now, a searing tightening in her head that made her knees almost buckle. The girl let herself be guided back to the Mustang, mumbling incoherently. In the car, her eyes closed and her body went slack, but the muttering continued.

"Snob! Snobby driving cunt . . . They won't get him, goddamn whores. Don't you understand? He's meant to be with me. Pack of goddamn whores."

By the time B. found a motor lodge, the girl was comatose. The night manager said nothing as B. paid in advance, parting with her precious bank bills, and then watched as if he had seen it all before B. lift the girl to her feet, string the brown arm around her shoulders and drag her to the room. She dumped the girl on a bed still in the dress. The girl looking now like a beat-up doll, face placid, hair askew, eyeliner wiped up her cheek.

B. kicked off her heels and went into the bathroom. She put her hands to her forehead against the spinning. In the mirror she saw her reflection: blackened eyes, greasy hair, pieces of sunburned skin flaking from her shoulders. Slowly, in a trance, she began peeling away the dead patches of skin. She peeled until her shoulders were raw, until translucent patches curled in the sink.

When she came out of the bathroom, the girl was up. She was squatted next to the bed flicking cigarette ash onto the carpet, mumbling again. The powder-blue dress lay crumpled on the floor. She was not wearing any shirt or underpants, just the jean cutoffs with her knees jutted out so her pubic hair showed, her small breasts two white circles against her brown tan, her eyelids fluttering open and closed. She had tried and failed, it appeared, to put on the turquoise leather choker—it lay over her shoulder, ties hanging down. ("I got it from an Indian lady at a concert. The real-deal stuff, no fakes.") B. noticed then the girl was wearing the bone-colored heels. Squatting naked in the bone-colored heels. With a surge of anger, B. shoved the girl on her bottom, yanked off the heels and threw them across the room. "I sa' put back on my own clothez," the girl slurred, up on her elbows, breasts upright. "Mise own clothes better."

B. pulled the girl up from the floor and pushed her back on the bed, flipping the bedspread to cover the dark nipples. "Go to sleep!" she yelled. The girl closed her eyes, her expression instantly serene. It was only then B. realized she must have taken something with the beers. Some hippie tab or root. B. retrieved the heels and, face hot, brushed them harshly with her fingers, as if this would remove the dirt and gouges. She hid them under her bed. She shook out the powder-blue dress and laid it over the television.

She went to the knapsack.

She took out the crumpled *LIFE* magazine, the wedding dress stained and the couple's faces now ripped beyond recognition. The carsickness was in every part of her body again, crushing her like a vice. She dropped the magazine in the trash.

It was a juvenile kind of writing in the notebook, bubbled letters and hearts dotting the i's. The entries just like the script, childish, stolid, complaints about her parents and Fontana, about Jed and the other women. This one was a "square," that one was a "phony," "a goddamn bummer." There was a creased flyer for a rock concert with obscene doodling. A list of highs, ranked.

Halfway through the girl had written an essay. The type a student might write for a junior high school English class, with centered underlined title: Why I liked the Governer's [sic] Mansion. "The pretty cups for tea," "a place for quiet for the governer to think." "What did you learn from this experience?" the girl wrote in conclusion. "Everyone needs his proper home."

B. clutched the page. Inside the crushing an inexplicable sadness rose. She thought of her own essay, what could it say. Why I Like the Valley. "The sights, the agriculture . . . The variety of the region's banks . . . The nothingness, the non-walks, the erasing heat . . . the driving . . . To keep driving."

She dropped the notebook to the floor. Still in a trance, she went to the knapsack and pulled out the suede vest, heavy with tobacco and body odor and musk. She unzipped her dress and stepped out, unhooked her bra. With the vest she hung a string of painted wooden beads around her neck. She placed one of the feathers in her knotted hair. The girl's blue jeans were too small over her hips; she sat in her underwear and lit one of the girl's cigarettes.

She tried to hum the rock song. The man's silky smug words commanding her not to hesitate, not to wallow. She got up and found the antler bone in her purse and sat with it in her lap. She tried inside the violent spinning to daydream: she was on the side of the highway, thinking of Andalusia, of the Indians, unconcerned, uninhibited, waiting for nothing, expectant of everything. Free.

The spinning broke through all of it. The drumming nausea. Her breasts sagged against the vest. She dug her nails into her palms. She tried to recite some of the Indian prayer. It was ridiculous. It was impossible.

The girl had come too late. The girl and her chants and her looseness. The sadness pooled at the bottom of the spinning. She lay down on the floor. The antler tumbled off. She stroked her cheek back and forth against the carpet. The only thing was the banks. The only irrefutable truth. Lying on the carpet she heard the *tick tick tick* of the clocks above the vault, the whoosh of paper across the counters.

26.

SHE WOKE WITH A THICK, confused feeling, as if she'd slept while everyone else had stayed awake. Her mouth tasted like ash. The sun was trying to break through in futile hatches in the drapes.

B. lifted herself up. Somewhere in the night she had crawled to her bed. She made out the form of the girl watching her in silence. B. stumbled out of bed and grabbed the powder-blue dress off the television and went into the bathroom. As she sat on the toilet she felt the carsickness saturate every pore, juddering and expanding as she wiped herself, as she stood up. The force of it renewed as though it had only been quietly metastasizing. She dug her nails into her palms.

When she came out, the girl was watching television, the smoke from her cigarette twisting in spectral columns in the dimness.

Her hair was still half in and half out of its bun, but otherwise she looked no worse for wear. As if the night had been B.'s personal hallucination.

"Whatever you're doing, I want in," the girl said.

She was inscrutable in the smoke, staring at the television.

B. did not answer.

"My mom collects these figurines," the girl went on. "All porcelain with gold at the edges, Little Bo Peeps and farmers and squirrels." She paused with a cool, almost clinical expression. "She puts them in a glass case and dusts them every day. Goes to work and comes home and doesn't talk to my dad, just rearranges the figurines. I don't want any figurines, any cement factory, any goddamn pools. But you need money to be free, don't you? You need money to get away. I want money, for Jed and me."

The girl's voice like a metal ringing in B.'s skull. The banks arranged themselves in her mind, the long fluorescent lights and neat rows of teller windows and evenly spaced islands for filling out forms. She wanted the girl to shut up so she could be alone with the images.

But the girl would not shut up. "I had my first diaphragm when I was fifteen and when my mother found it, she thought it was a strainer. For tea. *Didn't even know what it was.* Jed says it's a conspiracy they've been feeding us, like cyanide on our corn flakes."

"Like arsenic on corn flakes."

"Anyway, whatever you're doing, I want in. I want in on the action." The metal ringing hammering out in waves.

"I need coffee," B. said.

Outside, the day glared hot and smoggy yellow. Was it still July? B. did not know. In the office she poured herself a cup of coffee as the woman at the counter openly stared at her. "We're paid up," B. said. The woman did not even nod, just continued to stare.

The girl kept up her diatribe in the car. "The only person I'd marry is Jed, but we don't have those hangups." B. wondered if the girl had seen the *LIFE* magazine in the trash. The girl lit a new cigarette, marijuana this time. "We don't need it because I'm his old lady and he's my old man."

"And he's sleeping with other girls right now."

"You can goddamn take that back." The girl jabbed the joint at B., her hair slipping from the half-bun as she spoke. "That's none of your goddamn business."

They drove in silence for a while, the grass smoke acrid in the car.

"I'm not a prostitute," B. said finally.

"What then? You deal? My dealer in Fontana drives a yellow Corvette and could get us into the hippest shows in L.A. You don't seem the type."

"I'm not doing anything."

The girl sighed, the same sigh B. imagined she gave when her mother misconstrued the diaphragm. "Fine, you're not doing anything. You're just here with a stack of bills under your seat, driving around the valley picking up girls for charity."

"And there are blood stains," the girl said. "On the floor-board."

They drove through low green fields. B. no longer cared about classifying the crops. She felt somewhere in her reeling a need to make the girl stop her crazy ideas, to make her understand. "I like the banks," B. said. "I like the colors and the furniture and the people. They're safe and quiet. It's not for the money."

"So work in a bank."

"You're missing the point," B. said.

"I'm getting the point alright," the girl said. "It's called rob-bing banks. Checks, right? 'Cause I don't see you pulling this off with a gun and mask. Jed tried to pass a check once and they were on him in two seconds flat. But I can see that angle being right up your alley. The diamond and the heels and the hair and all. I can see that being exactly your thing."

"Why haven't you done any with me? Did they catch you or something?" the girl went on without missing a beat. "Well they won't recognize me."

"I could help you," she said. "I could help with your sickness or whatever."

For a moment, the idea held B. Someone to take away the affliction, to lay her down and pat her hair and tell her stories. But the girl's tired face and disordered hair hardened in front of her and B. knew this girl possessed no such balm.

The teller windows returned to her. The perfect squares of wood and glass, the soothing ivory walls. She must get rid of the girl.

The girl was still at it. "I see how the whole lady getup is the angle now. I can do that, like last night. I can do the lady thing, no problem."

"The dresses are dirty," B. protested. "They're too big."

"You said last night it fit perfectly," the girl retorted. B. suddenly understood her as the druggist had, something out of a German fairytale, vicious and hungry, not to be let in the door.

"I'm not asking for fifty-fifty. Whatever's fair. Any bread will help. For me and Jed, for our trip."

"We'll do the next one together," the girl was saying. "We can trade off. I'll do it and you can see how good I am and then you decide how much. And if you don't, I'll report you."

Everything was moving in its own dreamy, gel-like substance inside the carsickness. "I want to see the gold rush park first," B. said. "The one the man at the gas station told us about." She felt inexplicably that the gold rush park was the next step in the journey: the girl's threat, her chatter, the park—all of them ripples inside the thick, surreal wave that would get her back to the banks. No need for any plan. Now she understood. The banks were the only plan.

"Bunch of hicks came and missed the gold, got syphilis and died, the end."

"I want to see the park first," B. said implacably. "I don't care what we do after that."

"Fine. It's your trip. But don't stall on me."

B. took the small road back to the freeway. She pointed the car in the direction of the foothills. Leaving the valley now had its own part in the dream-gel logic. The girl chatted on, almost nervously, about how she'd stolen from five and dimes and corner stores since she was little. B. flattened the girl's voice into a distant hum. The slope rose almost imperceptibly as they drove, and then all of a sudden they were in the foothills, the anise scent in the bleached grasses and the hunched oak trees and the valley behind remote and blurred.

There were no landmarks near the sign. B. parked in the shadeless lot near a few picnic tables. The heat sucked instantly inside the car. She gathered her purse and sat for a moment, looking out the window. "I won't be long," she said. The girl said nothing.

At the park entrance, a ranger stood in a shack. A transistor radio crackled behind him, the baseball game organ scaling up and down, the cheers of the crowd listless ripples in the heat. Under the man's ranger hat he wore dark wraparound glasses so that B. couldn't see his eyes. "It's self-guided," he said, handing her a pamphlet. "Over a hundred years of state history in one park, ma'am. Happy prospecting." A languid cheer whined from the game.

A lizard with no tail skittered in front of her. A series of small signs appeared along the trail: "Ten thousand men crowded the bank here in search of a dream. But the dream was elusive." The signs went on about claims and sluice boxes and the few who struck any gold and the multitudes who left destitute. The women were cooks and madams. B. remembered reading that somewhere.

She came to a stack of pans by the river, apparently for trying your own hand at panning. She picked one up and removed the bone-colored heels and climbed slowly into the freezing water. The cold woke her up out of the dream-gel substance, made her sharp and lucid inside the spinning. She moved into the water. The edges of the cut on her foot gilled. She bent down and shoveled up the dirt and shook it around the pan. Nothing. She dumped and tried again, shimmying the rocks and sand and coming up empty again, her hands turning blue in the icy water. She tried once more, the sharp buzzing in her head and throat. It would be easy to keep trying it all day, she saw, to go on hoping and waiting for something to appear. In frustration she tossed the pan into the water and watched it float away. She walked out of the river to one of the oaks and sat. From her spot she saw the girl get out of the car, climb onto a picnic table, light a cigarette and lie back in the sun. B. shivered. She reached into the ostrich-skin purse reflexively for a check, forgetting they were in the glove compartment. Instead she came up with the knife from the buttes.

She examined it for a long moment. Its sleekness was

comforting to hold. She angled the blade so the sun glinted off and it gave her a feeling of sudden reassurance, as if she could reach into her purse and find whatever she needed. She leaned against the oak tree and let the comfort of the knife wash over her.

When she got back to the Mustang, the girl was in her seat with the door open, feet on the concrete, painting her nails with B.'s nail polish.

"You hit the motherlode?" The girl did not look up from her strokes. Her long hair was out of the bun now and back in her face. The bubblegum pink did not obscure the dirt in her nails. B. walked to the driver's side without responding.

"We should do it now," the girl said then. "Strike while the iron's hot." She was brushing out a last line of her big toe, swabbing the remnants with her fingernails.

B. was still at the oak tree, on a calm plane above the girl. "I don't think it's a good idea," she answered.

"I didn't ask whether it was a good idea," the girl snapped. "If you don't let me, I'll turn you in."

The absurdity of the conversation, the threat, did not touch B. She started the engine and backed out before the girl could move. "Shit, let me close the door!" The girl scrambled to get her feet in. After that, the girl remained silent for a while, having sensed the shift in mood. They drove down a two-lane road from the park and at the first gas station, B. turned in.

"You can change in the bathroom," B. said.

"I need you to help me," the girl said.

In the single restroom with its urinal and green flickering light, B. pulled the powder-blue dress out of the travel bag and thrust it at the girl. She got out her makeup case and haphazardly brushed eye shadow and mascara and blush onto the tan face.

"You can't wear my heels anymore."

"Why not?"

B. ignored her. "We'll go to the nearest town with a store and a bank and get you your own shoes."

"I'm not paying."

B. yanked the girl's hair back into a chignon as best she could. The girl said nothing, just stared at her face in the green-lit mirror, in the warm smell of urine and mothballs.

In the car, the girl began talking nervously again.

"It's just that I don't have those housewife hang-ups, you know. He's free, I'm free. But if I come back with the bread, well, the groupies can't give him that." She absentmindedly smoothed the wrinkled lap of the dress as she spoke.

The next town they reached was two short blocks, a Mexican restaurant and an insurance shop on one side, a fabrics and sewing supply store on the other. Next to that a clothing store. B. parked in front. She noticed as she got out that the girl was still wearing an anklet, a strip of dark leather with hanging white shells. The girl should have taken off the anklet. "Wait here, I don't want them to see you," B. said. In the clothing store, there were outfits for everyone and everything—overalls, wedding dresses, toddlers' rompers. A crescent-shaped display of shoes for all occasions. B. chose a pair of white pumps in her own size.

The saleswoman boxed up the shoes, offering tips for the stains on B.'s dress ("Little bit of selzer, little bit of baking soda, that'll come right off."), but B. was fixated on the anklet. It spoiled the calm from the gold rush park. The confusion of dark leather and shells and the powder-blue dress, the incongruity everywhere.

"You need to take that off," she said slowly in the car. "Take it off if you're going to do it right."

The girl slipped on the heels and turned them this way and that on the dashboard admiring, the shells clicking. "Got that from the Indian lady too. It's good luck."

All at once B. remembered the antler bone on the motel room floor. Gone, no luck anywhere.

"You can't wear that with the heels," she told the girl.

"Relax," the girl said. "Don't worry so much. They'll never see."

The bank was at the end of a two-block street. The girl had already retrieved the checkbook from the glove compartment, ripped one out and written on it with her bubbled writing. She stepped out of the car without a word. B. watched the long solid back of the powder-blue dress, set off by the girl's tan, the white pumps and the anklet. They disappeared through the glass doors.

On the road she had thought again of a house. With the girl. This time far up at the northern edge of the valley, where she'd never been, hundreds of miles away from the realtors and beauty salons and university men. The afternoon light in the windows as clear to her as if she'd seen it in person. A grove of eucalyptus and orange trees in back. A porch. And the girl in the afternoon light. "Come with me to a house," B. had imagined saying in this fantasy. "Come with me and we can sort things out."

When the girl sat back in the car, B. had the knife ready. She stuck the point at the girl's ribs.

"Take the money and move on."

The girl sat momentarily stunned. Then she tried to turn. B. pressed the knife further in.

"Fuck you and your twisted Donna Reed show," the girl finally whispered. She grabbed the knapsack and got out of the car and kicked off the white pumps and threw them at the door.

"You crazy old cunt!"

B. did not look back. She imagined the girl barefoot in the anklet and powder-blue dress, receding.

THE ROAD SEEMED A SERIES of waves moving her forward. She drove past billboards for casinos and ski resorts (like a practical joke in the heat) and knew she was heading into the mountains. She wondered for a moment if the girl might report her but decided she would not risk being shipped back to Fontana. B.

thought of the girl's mother—intent over the porcelain, dusting the petticoats, waiting for the girl to return. B. laid on the gas. The car sloped up and up, she could see the pines ahead. Surrounding her on all sides the spots of oak, gentle and lulling, drawing her on. She would tell the girl's mother how she had tried to visit the bridge, to sit in the mission chapel, to take in the hummingbirds and crocuses. But that only the banks had worked. The carsickness was a violent and spinning nausea as she drove. B. imagined the girl's mother would understand. Who had worn the kid gloves and sat for the wash-and-sets. Who had lost the daughter with the long loose hair and bare feet. *What have you learned from this experience?* The vault clocks ticked through B.'s mind. She saw she could just continue on, higher into the mountains, until she was through. Until she was out.

She skidded to a stop in the middle of the road. The gentle bending grass alongside her and the dark jagged mountains ahead.

She brought the steering wheel around its column, turning the car in one single movement onto the shoulder and back in the other direction. Back into the valley.

27.

In an all-night laundromat, she drank a bottle of Coke from a machine. She put the cool glass between her legs. Out of the foothills her crotch had begun itching violently and in the ladies' room at the laundromat, she'd discovered a forgotten last tampon. How many days? She no longer knew. Since before the night with the university professor. Forgetting this necessary feminine ceremony, and so it had been inadvertently rammed inside her and left to fester there, disintegrating, gathering its bacteria. She dug for several minutes for the string. The tampon halted on the way out, dry and bloated to twice its size, making her wince. She washed her fingers raw with the powdered soap. On the lip of the sink she had fanned out the bills (she'd collected everything from under the front seat, finding the sweaty cellophane-wrapped doughnuts too). She did not want to count the bills but to separate out the newest ones and roll these into her bra strap as she had that first day, understanding now their power as a totem next to her skin. Back in her blue plastic seat, she tensed her thighs together to stop the itching but it raged. The only other person in the laundromat was a woman folding endless pairs of shorts, some the size of napkins, and B. thought momentarily of striking up some conversation, but a slovenly aspect in the woman—a burst seam in her pedal pushers, a missing button on her blouse—made B. avoid her. She was too tired to drive to a motel. She preferred to sit and watch the suds in the washer tumble and churn. She might even plan a route as she watched, map out how she could conduct the banks in a prudent and logical manner this time, strategically.

But as she watched, the swirling liquid turned gray . . . the gray of the city . . . the gray of the fog. And suddenly she was back a few days before the first check. The day when the fog had never lifted, the day she'd left work early to settle her electric bill in person (her electricity turned off, the payment—was it two?—forgotten, when normally she stayed so on top of those things, on things like bill paying and facial masks). The fog had never lifted that day, hanging in gray veils between buildings. There was a buzzing at the back of her neck that had begun in the morning but she'd managed to contain it with typing and filing to a thin steady drone. As she walked the concrete canyons and could not find the bus stop, the droning got worse. The one-dimensional light brightening and deadening objects at the same time to a flat nothingness. She hurried past two drifters on a corner, a man with a guitar in striped pants and a woman in a tall, sinister bowler hat handing out carnations. When B. finally found the stop, shivering in her navy bouclé suit, she stood next to a pretty young woman and felt relief.

And yet on closer inspection, the young woman had worn no stockings, her hair long and frizzy, braless under the paisley dress. Carrying not a handbag or gloves but a satchel across her chest and a thick textbook titled *Advanced Microbiology* in her arm. Not a drifter and yet not anything B. had ever known before, not anything she recognized. For the first time with the carsickness she vomited. Retched onto the sidewalk. The girl tried to offer some help, but B. stumbled away and found a taxi, mailed the check to the utility company and lived for the rest of the week with candles.

"Where's the nearest bank?" B. asked the woman folding laundry, turning away from the gray suds.

The woman explained and it seemed to B. that she understood exactly why B. had asked. She understood the gray suds and the girl at the bus stop and that the banks were the only answer.

———•———

SHE BOUGHT BABY POWDER FOR her hair so she would not have to wash it. She remembered from college that cranberry juice helped the itching and bought two jars and drank them as she drove. The lipstick was also essential, the lipstick with the diamond brooch and the French twist (with the baby powder). She carefully applied a pink or a coral right before she went in, just as she carefully held down her shoulders and put on a smile and nodded during small talk. In the motels, while she still used them, she hung up the ivory sheath and slept in her bra and underwear. But when she began sleeping in the Mustang—in order to hoard more bills, and because she was not sleeping much anyway—she kept the dress on. It now had creases like cuts in it and an unmistakably sour stain of sweat. In truck-stop restrooms she forced herself to wash her armpits. (Some aspect of stepping into a shower would undo everything. She used the restroom soap just enough to cover her smell.) There was of course the light green poplin she had not even worn yet. But the ivory was now a talisman, a marker of some kind. The bone-colored heels were now a light brown.

Three a day was the most she managed because of the long distances. Her best one of the first, when she'd fallen into extended small talk with a teller about the preferred route to Tahoe, the girl emphatic about taking Highway 50 to avoid the trucks and come out on the south side. The girl's passion for the distinction, her engrossment in the nuances—the importance of ending up at the casinos, for example—allowing B. time to absorb the straight lines, the subdued voices, the browns and beiges. The cool expansive feeling had lasted and lasted. She had not needed a second bank. That day she had parked under a eucalyptus break and slept peacefully in the shade all afternoon.

But as the days passed, the cool expansive feeling began to lessen. She attributed this first to mitigating factors: the bank that had been near a canning plant and so polluted with the awful tang of stewed tomatoes she could not take anything else in. Another where she'd become so distracted by her dirty fingernails—the black against the chipped pink—that she'd forgotten her opening bit about the weather and signed her own name on the check. (The teller had not noticed.) And even when it went off all right, the cool expansive feeling evaporated after a few minutes. Like a drug with no kick. The spinning and nausea returned fiercer than before, making her gun the engine for the next town and the next one after that.

The spree lasted five days, until the morning she walked into the bank and saw the small poster with the sketch. ATTRACTIVE BLONDE, EARLY THIRTIES, 5'7", 120 POUNDS, WEARS DIAMOND BROOCH. Even then she had considered continuing on to the counter, filling out one of the last checks, until a reflex finally kicked in and she walked out.

28.

AT A GAS STATION SHE bought a coffee and a doughnut to keep herself alert. She fingered her bra strap. There were too many bills to fit them all in there now: she had stuffed the rest into the ostrich-skin purse and back under the seat of the Mustang, as if surrounding herself with a protective force field. The gas station attendant eyed her as she nibbled the icing. She touched her hair; the baby powder had stopped absorbing the grease. She moved casually away from the door.

She walked behind the station. The mountains were no longer even visible in the brown haze, the valley an endless plain. At her feet everywhere were the wild poppies. Her brain pressed out against her skull, against the backs of her eye sockets. The neon-orange clusters in the dead dry grass pulsed at her. She chucked the coffee and doughnut and followed railroad tracks.

The buzzing of the electrical wires like the whir in her head, the trash transmuting itself into diamonds and roses. She yanked a clutch of poppies. Like yanking out the incongruities, the inexplicable. She walked, mashing and dropping the petals, trying to see how she had got here, what to do next.

It had not seemed, as it now did, inevitable: She had risen that day like any other, slipped on the ivory sheath and pinned her hair. She had chosen the bone-colored heels to match the sheath and not taken a sweater for the fog because she was tired of wearing sweaters in July. She had picked up a newspaper to read before and after the bus (because of the motion sickness) and she had made it all as it usually was, even after the girl at the bus stop had made her vomit, even after her mother had called her a lesbian. She read the newspaper but inside was a picture of a burning city in the East. The picture not of the police with shields or the people carrying off televisions, but of a group of black women at a police station. Bags under their eyes, deadened gazes, curlers in their hair, waiting. B. stood in the wet morning air, shivering without a sweater, riveted. She tried to scan other headlines: landslides in Japan and the stock market down. But the black women waiting remained. They were some kind of portent, a communiqué to her alone. The wave of nausea nearly buckled her. She dropped the newspaper in the trash and staggered onto the bus when it came. She gripped her seat. She knew she would not vomit again; she would not get off so easily. Across from her a Chinese woman with the short mannish hair, a suited man reading his paper. She grasped in her mind for a soothing memory, her mother demonstrating the proper method of folding a dress shirt. Collar down, shoulders indented, buttons pressed. B. moved her hands quietly in this rhythm, collar down, shoulders indented, buttons pressed. But the suited man, whom she'd seen day in and day out, with his paper cup of coffee and shiny gold band, small, balding, who never looked up from his paper, struck her, and she put it together: it was this or some other man's dress shirt she was folding in her mind. The bus rattled under electric wires. The weekend to come again, the hours to be counted, and the only thing to be done to fold the suited man's dress shirt in one's mind. (While he went off to work with his coffee and paper, day after day, as if nothing was wrong, as if B. were not ill and the black women not waiting and the young women not loose-clothed and long-haired at bus stops.) At her stop, B. stumbled off and into her office building and at her desk she turned on the typewriter and typed the first letter in her basket without removing her purse from her wrist, and then another, and then another. The spinning on and on.

Without thinking, she reached in her purse for one of the counterfeit checks she'd not yet dared touch. And like the detonating of a bomb the thoughts *stopped*.

She left her desk with the typewriter still humming. The bank a block away the oldest in the West, a plaque certified, and the brass fixtures shone and the glass panes lined up perfectly across the marble. There was nothing to focus on but the gleam and the panes and the softness of the teller's hair, and there was no going back.

Out of her palm fell the crushed poppies. A train whistle blew in the near distance. She left the railroad tracks and walked back to the Mustang and understood exactly where to go next.

29.

AN OCHEROUS AFTERNOON LIGHT FELL on the subdivision.
B. drove past the gate, the colored flags flat in the dead air.
The stucco houses looked blanched in the heat, which seemed
to radiate up from the ground and in from fields and to bend
the new trees along the street to nowhere. She parked the car
and walked into the cul-de-sac. Her brain continuing to press
against her skull. A toddler on a tricycle in a faded bathing suit
stared blankly at her.

B. passed the unfinished houses with giant still-empty
rooms and followed the walkway of the first occupied unit.
She glanced around. The toddler continued to stare. B. flipped
quickly through the letters, slipping anything official-looking
into the ostrich-skin purse. She did this at three more houses.
As she walked back to her car, the throbbing and swirling and

heat and caffeine came together in a steady blaring in her mind.

A man came out of one of the houses. "Are you looking for Patty? Because she's sick today." B. walked on without answering, past the little girl, fumbling with the car keys. The man followed her.

"I can have her call you! She'll hate to have missed—"

B. slammed the door of the Mustang and peeled out.

In a motel room with the drapes closed she opened the envelopes. She did not look at the amounts, just wrote down names and account numbers on a torn-out page of the phone book.

She dialed him. His face coalesced in her mind only in the vaguest form, black and pink dabs on a canvas.

He did not pick up. She lay her head on the bedspread, the heavy receiver at her ear. She dialed again and again. In the clicks and the tumbling she felt the carsickness drumming her down into a dark echoing pit.

When he finally answered, she said: "I'll tell you the truth this time."

Her mind focused on the single guiding image of the banks. "It's some trouble I got into back east. A loan I took out under the table."

There was silence on the line, the lighting of a cigarette. "Go on," he said.

She waited for the signal of the image in her mind. "It was an operation. I've never told anyone. I was pregnant, by one of the college boys. He proposed. But he hit me." She told him she'd gotten a backroom abortion but something had gone wrong; she'd had terrible pains. When she finally went to her doctor, he advised a hysterectomy.

It was a true story. She'd heard one of the secretaries tell it about a friend, except instead of having the operation the friend had hung herself by a belt in her closet.

She thought for a moment she'd lost him.

"So you couldn't tell your mama and papa who sent you to the nice little college to marry a nice little college boy," he said. But she heard in his voice the beginning of a desire to believe her.

"No."

"You already lied to me once."

"I'm not lying."

She waited to hear cigarette paper crumpling, an exhale. She heard nothing.

Finally, he spoke. "I'm sorry that happened to you. It's not right something like that should happen to you."

"Will you help me then?"

She felt his vulnerability beating through the line. "What's in it for me?" he asked.

"I'll be your girl, Daughtry."

She considered briefly how she was deceiving him. But the dark sinking pulled her down and she knew there was only one thing she cared about.

30.

He was waiting for her in the lobby of a new Motel 6 off the freeway. As he walked through the glass doors she saw that he was unshaven, his thick black eyebrows unruly as if he had tossed and turned and left straight from bed. He told her to walk toward the Mustang with him and they sat in the front seats without looking at each other.

"I have new account numbers," B. blurted out.

"What are you talking about?"

"I took them from a subdivision."

He put his forehead in his hands. "You kidding me? Are you asking to get caught? It's not as big as you think out here. You have to let me take care of that."

"I wanted to be prepared. So it would go more quickly."

"How did you know I'd help you, huh? You think I'm a sucker?" She tried not to hear the plaintiveness in his voice.

"Of course not," she stalled. "I was just hoping. I was hoping you'd see me again. I wanted it to help us."

"Forget the damn account numbers."

A brown-skinned maid rolled her cart in front of the car. In a torturous slowness, she pulled out one at a time a roll of toilet paper, a set of sheets, soap. B. tried to wait but could not. "Do you have the new ones?"

He kneaded the eyebrows. "I could leave right now. Sob story and all."

"Will it take very long, Daughtry?"

"I could, you know. Get back in the car and drive all the damn way back and forget I ever met you."

"Please help me, Harold."

He turned toward the door and rubbed his knuckles across his cheek. He looked all of a sudden small and thin.

"We'll have them in a day," he said coldly. "My buddy'll deliver them here. He wants a cut."

"We could go meet him," she said.

He laughed angrily. "Ha! You ain't the one making the deals." He reached across her and opened the passenger door. "C'mon."

He led her to his own car in the parking lot. It was a battered coupe, the black interior faded to gray, a piece of ceiling hanging, gouges in the seats. It smelled of cigarettes and aftershave. She did not like leaving the Mustang, but she knew she must follow him. When she'd woken up that morning, her muscles had been taut with dizziness, her fingers clenched around the bedspread, numb.

He drove out behind the motel, toward a collection of cottonwood trees in a vacant field. Their appearance in the middle of the empty lot gave them the aspect of a solemn gathering, a mournful tête-à-tête. "I saw this spot driving in," he said. "We can relax a little, be normal for once. It'll be good for you. You don't look right." From the trunk of the coupe he grabbed a bag of sandwiches and six-pack of beer and she noted with passing guilt that he had made a picnic for her.

The creek under the cottonwoods was a bed of dry rocks. He laid out his black leather blazer for her to sit on and spread out the sandwiches. His oiled hair was a dark dome over his pale face, his features pale and tired and slicked with sweat from the heat. B. drank some of the beer but did not feel like touching the sandwich in the hot shade. She wanted to get the picnic over with, act through whatever Daughtry needed her to act through, get on to the checks. But Daughtry smoked a cigarette and drank his beer in sullen silence, as if mulling over a lost argument. The beer and the heat brought her back to her girlhood, her father with his bottle in the backyard after pruning and watering the roses (he loved to tend the rosebushes, never her mother). He spoke to B. in the simplest of terms—what she was playing, where she and her mother had bought her dress—and she did not know why she missed these stunted exchanges, why they seemed now reassuringly delineated.

She knew she should try to tell Daughtry about missing the delineation, to offer some kind of truth. "I suppose when I was a girl," she began hesitatingly, "I had the same idea about growing up as everyone else. Marriage, children. Then in college I didn't want to think about it. I only wanted to be on my own for a while, have my own apartment and job, nothing seemed so urgent . . . Then people started making less sense. They always asked me the same things. They started to feel very different from me, from what I thought about, and I began . . . to feel funny. I had this dizziness, you see, this nausea or wooziness or I don't know how to describe it. So I tried to feel better from what's supposed to make a girl feel better: meeting men, seeing pretty flowers, having my hair done. But none of it worked. And now the dizziness is there all the time. It never stops." She gasped for air, it seemed. "Sometimes I don't see how to live."

Daughtry took a long pull on his beer and then tossed the empty can toward the dry creek. "Tell you the truth, part of me wants to hit you. I've never hit a girl and I never will, but part of me wants to slap some sense into you so bad I could taste it.

"You got no idea what it's like, with your school and your books and your fanciness. It's not like I don't have dreams too, you know. I'm a *custodian*, for Chrissakes . . . I want to get a little fishing boat. My days off sometimes I go down near the wharves and throw in a line, take the catch back to Chinatown and sell 'em right outta the bucket. Gone in minutes, those Chinamen know their fish. But it makes me feel good. I got my own spot picked out and it don't matter if it's foggy and the tourists are shaking in their windbreakers, I'm out there and I don't have to think about the damned union or time card or parole. Just the smell of the ocean and the fog mixed in the air, like a perfume . . . I can smell it here in this dry hole. Now if I had a boat, that's all I'd do.

"I'm sorry you're dizzy," he said. "But you've never had to worry about money in your life. I knew that the first day I saw you. You could do anything."

"Have you ever been on a boat, Daughtry?"

He dug at the dry grass with his boot heel. "Naw. But I seen 'em doing it. I could do it if I had the chance."

He looked up into the cottonwoods. He seemed to be reading the flickering leaves for some go-ahead.

"I thought about it the whole drive out here. What I think we should do. That would really set us up, fix us both. By the time we're done we'll have enough to get to Mexico, and I think we should get married down there." He paused here but still did not look down from the trees. "You told me yourself the college guy hurt you, and so that kind of guy isn't the answer for you. You need someone like me. You're too soft for things, is what I've figured out. Too thin-skinned. I'm the kind of guy who can look out for you." His voice gathered strength as he spoke. "So after this run, we won't have to do anything else. I can get a boat down there and take care of us. You're different and I'm different and maybe we fit together."

He paused and there was a hot breeze rustling the cotton-wood leaves, then silence.

"You can say right now if you don't want to marry me and I'll leave you alone." He looked at her now. "I'll leave you alone, but you'll be on your own getting the money. That's my offer to you."

She had watched his mouth moving, his tobacco-stained teeth and his pointed tongue flashing periodically over his dry lips. The words "marriage" and "Mexico" floated over her. She understood in them only her hands at the counters again, sliding the checks forward and collecting back the crisp bills, returning to the delineations, the cool expansive feeling. She would tell him whatever he needed to hear.

"I can't cook," she answered finally.

A crooked smile bloomed in his face. "I'll handle it, baby. I'll do the fishing and the cooking and you just stay pretty and get a tan." He grabbed her and pressed her head into the damp of his chest, lips to her dirty hair. "It'll be the best living. You'll see."

She waited in the odor of his undershirt and their sweat for him to release her. The dappling of light through the cotton-woods made parts of them golden, his bicep, her white wrist, and in this light his proposal and her acceptance of it were remote and enchanted, a story she could listen to and admire.

Back at the motel, he threw an envelope onto the bed. The

blonde woman in the new driver's license had not dissimilar features—an oval face, the aquiline nose. But the woman's eyes were younger, fresh and open. B. memorized the freshness before putting the ID into the ostrich-skin purse, as if she could inhabit that too.

Daughtry made love to her in the motel bed. He did not comment on her rankness, the rat's nest French twist; it seemed to make him that much more devouring. She tried to lose herself in the sensations of skin on skin, the friction and release. But in reality she was walking across the linoleum, taking up the chained ballpoint pen, watching the clock above the vault. He fell asleep afterward, his hot thick body clamped over hers, but she went on, tracing the lines of the teller windows, running her fingers along the velvet ropes.

31.

IN THE MORNING, HE MADE her shower and wash her hair. "We gotta get you dolled up the way I first saw you," he said. She shrunk under the water as if the drops burned her skin. She made no move to lather or scrub. But Daughtry was waiting. She knew he would make her do it again. She forced herself to soap a washcloth and pass it over her body once, to pour out shampoo and rub it through her hair.

Daughtry appraised her in the mirror as she applied her makeup. He got out the diamond brooch from her bag (she did not ask how he'd known it was there). She did not want to alarm him by telling him about the flyer. "I think that's too formal for day, don't you?" she said. He shrugged. The green poplin dress was laid out on the bed. "But I want to wear the ivory," she said. "Baby, that's a godawful mess, no offense. You look rundown in that." He held out the green and when she did not immediately take it, he did not lower his arm. When she finally took it, she knew already it was wrong: the color too bright, the poplin too flimsy, the girlish belling of the skirt. Pulling her back somewhere she did not want to go. He brushed his fingers across her forehead and she forced herself not to flinch.

"We'll get you new dresses, baby. All brand new."

They went back to the lobby of the Motel 6 and a short wiry man with a blond goatee was waiting, wearing in the heat a buttoned-up dark denim jacket like Daughtry wore his leather blazer. Daughtry had B. stay outside on the hot asphalt where she shifted in the green dress, feeling conspicuous, watching the goateed man and Daughtry enact the mime of exchanging an envelope and shaking hands under the orbed hanging lamps of the lobby. The smell of hot tar from the parking lot sharpened the carsickness.

They took the Mustang. Daughtry sat in the driver's seat without asking.

"Can I see the checks?" she asked.

He laughed. "When we get there, doll. Just hold your horses."

She distracted herself by counting the rows of crops and fruit trees. But they went too quickly and the telephone poles too slowly and she could not block out Daughtry rambling on about the fishing "down South." The only thing she could do to escape the growing of ill portent (not holding the checks, the green poplin dress) was to close her eyes and pretend to sleep.

But she felt the dread still behind her eyelids. Before she knew it they were parked in front of a cinder-block building hedged by pruned oleanders, the sun glaring off its silver-coated doors. She had a moment's hesitation that she'd already been to this bank. She decided she had not.

"Can I see them now?" B. asked.

"Sure, baby." Daughtry handed over the vinyl book but watched her with it as if she were a small child handling a delicate ornament. She ran her fingers over the paper, studying the lines, the block address and cool blue pattern, the name to match the fake license.

"You know what to do?" he asked.

This struck her as funny and she laughed the first genuine laugh she could remember in months, until she saw his injured expression. She patted his hand and told him she knew and got out.

The entire length of her rushed with blood. She felt as she walked toward the entrance that her skin needed only to be brushed up against for her to explode. But the bad signal came immediately in her reflection in the glass door. The light green and belling skirt. When she swung open the door the air inside was too cold. The ivory on the walls not soothing but dull, the line of teller windows a row of draining rectangles and the empty desks pointless.

She made her way to the middle island. She jerkily filled out a withdrawal form; she crumpled it and started over. She absentmindedly put her hand to her heart but the diamond brooch was not there. In the corners of the ceiling she noticed the security cameras for the first time.

The teller's perfume had hints of gardenia, bringing the Brylcreemed boy and the graduation luncheon briefly into her head. She made her way past the stiff bow tie and the white linens in her mind, concentrating to speak each word.

"I'd like to make this out to cash."

"You're from the city," the teller said (except it sounded like "thity" because of the girl's lisp).

"How did you know?" B. whispered.

"It says so on your check." Her lisp had disappeared. "And you don't look like you're from here," the girl said without a shadow of malice. Then the lisp returned: "Now just a minute, Miss Lawthon, I'll thee if we can accommodate this request."

The girl walked over to a manager at one of the empty desks. B. waited for her palms to dampen or her heart to race but no fear or anxiety was in her. Her body seemed to slacken, as if it were ready to be led away. But when the manager glanced over, his easy nod and smile showed that he had no qualms about her, the pretty patron with her clean dress and washed hair. The cool expansive feeling did come then. She thanked the teller and gathered the cash and walked out.

In the car, she presented the money to Daughtry. "Sweet Jesus. They practically handed you the reserves. Is this how easy it's been for you? We should do another, baby! While we're on a goddamn roll."

But by then the cool expansive feeling had already faded.

He drove them an hour north and when she did the next bank, an old stone building with ionic columns and octagonal-shaped lamps, it was the same easy success and the same fleeting cool expansive feeling. A siren rose faintly in her head. Like a careening from a distance, the pitch higher and higher but never arriving.

"C'mon, let's do another," Daughtry said. "Hell, I'm Irish, we know a thing or two about luck." He drove an hour southwest this time, babbling about Mexico on the way. ". . . and in the little fishing villages, you can live right on the cliffs. Right on the Pacific Ocean. Just like those Seventeen-Mile Drive bastards, except ours . . . They have a beautiful kind of tuna down there, baby, a gorgeous fish, tastes like steak and they swim around by the boatloads. And all the water warm as a bath, no fog, no cold . . . And then, baby, after we finish the season, we'll travel. We'll see the whole goddamned beautiful continent, the ruins and the jungles, and never think of this rat race again." B. heard him only intermittently through the siren. It blared behind her eyes now, rising to a shriek. It was white in her mind. She clutched the seat. She tried to focus on Daughtry's house at the sea but she could only glance at a pink adobe with birds of paradise and then watch it vanish.

At the last bank, she could not walk steadily. The shrill of the

siren bleaching everything to a white blur. Before she got as far
as the start of the line, she buckled. She got up before anyone
got near her and turned around. In the car, she told Daughtry
the same thing she told herself: she was too hungry and too
tired and it would go better in the morning.

Daughtry took her to a steakhouse they'd passed on the way
in. It was an old Victorian, with tall shutters and a porch edged in
scallops, stained floral wallpaper behind the leather booths and
chairs. Daughtry ordered her a T-bone with a side of spinach
and a martini. "You need iron. And you need a drink."

He smiled a wide dopey smile and grasped her hand. "I like
taking care of you," he said. Then he lowered his voice. "I want
to take care of you every night, baby. Every night I want to
make you feel good." Inside the siren B. could only nod at his
short yellow teeth.

He watched her eat. The grainy meat stuck in her throat, it
made her gag. She finished her martini and asked for another.
By the third round Daughtry stopped watching so closely and
the alcohol at least blunted the surface of the siren, letting the
churn continue deeper down. She waited until Daughtry got up
for the men's room and slid the rest of her steak into her napkin.
In the small opening created by the martinis, she tried to grasp at
the pink adobe house as a way to breathe. She tried to think rea-
sonably about a house again, to think about it in a way she had
not yet: she could go there with Daughtry. It might not be so
bad, she told herself. To learn to make fish soups, to embroider

festive blouses and arrange tropical flowers in vases. (She had no other vision of what she would do in the house.) Maybe she had been wrong about marriage. Perhaps this had been the answer all along—never the banks, never the checks. But as she told herself this, the siren drilled violently through the alcohol to the top of her skull. She seized the edge of the table, knocking over her martini. Gin dribbled onto the green dress. Somewhere inside the violent tilting, she knew *it would not matter if it was Daughtry or the Boston almost-fiancé or the university man or the developer and Sherry.* It would not matter who was in the pink adobe house with her, *she did not want to live in it with any of them.* She did not want to make fish soups. She did not want to be taken care of or to fix her hair. She wanted only to get away, to start over, to undo something that seemed to bind her. She wanted only to find a calm quiet place to breathe. The landscape of her daydreams, the blue-white featureless expanse.

Daughtry came back from the bathroom and slid beside her, nibbled her neck. His aftershave and sweat and meaty breath only vaguely penetrating the careening. Her fingertips were bloodless from gripping. She pressed herself against his chest and palmed his lapel pocket.

He snatched her hand. "What d'you need those for, huh? Don't you have enough here?" He leaned her back and wiped at the green dress with a napkin. "What d'you need those for right now?"

She sat immobile as he wiped her. "Get me out of here," she

whispered. Daughtry downed the rest of his martini, unfurled the new bills on the table and led her out by the elbow.

He made a point of locking the checks in the trunk of the Mustang, and in the motel room he dragged the mattress from the bed and shoved it against the door. "You're beat. We both need a good night's sleep without getting up drunk and having an accident." She lay down on the mattress and closed her eyes, as if this might have any effect on the siren. Daughtry held her to him. "The last thing I need—Christ, the very last thing—is kids. I see you worrying, and you don't have to. Not with me." He kissed her cheek.

He had never asked her how there could be no scar. No mark from the invented hysterectomy. He did not, she knew, really want to know.

"Shhh." She put her finger to her lips. "Let's just sleep." From her lock in his arms, she watched the shaft of yellow porch light through the curtains. She kept her eyes on the shaft of light for as long as she could.

32.

THE NEXT MORNING SHE HAD not slept. The siren had quieted but the spinning continued, the unnameable dread had grown with each hour. Daughtry had woken early while she'd pretended to be asleep to delay having to speak. He had gone out and brought back coffee and somehow acquired nail polish remover and a tortoiseshell plastic headband.

He insisted on another shower. Before she got in he wiped the ragged pink polish off nail by nail. "Better to have none than to look chipped. We can get you to one of those nail places later." Then he found a file in her travel bag (she was surprised to remember she owned such a thing) and cleaned out and filed her nails one by one.

She stood silent as he worked the plastic tortoiseshell into her hair. "To add class," he said. He stood back to admire her.

She was aware beyond the spinning and fatigue that the itching and burning in her crotch had returned. The sex with Daughtry had brought it back, like a chronic affliction.

"I need cranberry juice."

"Sure, baby," Daughtry said, but he was adjusting the headband in the mirror and not listening.

At breakfast, he made her eat half a doughnut and a few bites of egg, all of which choked in her throat. The restaurant had no cranberry juice.

She tried to steady herself by focusing on the Formica table. But the gold flecks jittered around like a frantic cosmos. "So this time try for a little more," Daughtry was saying. "You're looking good. You're looking like a living doll, you want to know the truth. They won't peg you. And the sooner we're done, the sooner we split."

Daughtry went on lauding their prospects. She reached into the ostrich-skin purse and absently touched the knife.

Inside the bank, she noted the two security cameras first and looked into each as if to acknowledge them. Then she made a check out to herself for $10,000.

The attractive brunette with hair teased into a bouffant smiled widely at B. "I'll just have to approve this with my manager," she said in a cheery voice.

B. nodded robotically. She did feel like a living doll, made up and ready.

A large man in a red tie and a sea-blue suit walked back

with the teller. "Have you checked this with anyone, ma'am? I wouldn't want you to overdraw the account." He stared at her from his plump face, quivering at the jowls.

"It's 'miss.' No, there's no one to check it with."

The man's doughy eyes did not move from her.

"It's a large amount," he said.

"It's what I want."

He coughed. The brunette teller stood at his side, smiling, pressing at a bobby pin in her hair, apparently unaware what was holding up the transaction.

"Excuse us for a moment," the manager said. He walked away. The teller remained a beat, still smiling, then followed him.

B. saw him talk to another man in a tie. She saw a security guard watch the two men talking, then watch her.

Something warm entered her then. It puzzled her at first. She felt it spread. Starting inside the spinning and moving through her entire body. A pleasurable, liquid sensation. A warm analgesia, but emanating from the carsickness. As if the nausea and whirling had beaten so violently inside her they'd mealed the element that still fought them into a warm, pliant pulp. Like alcohol in her veins.

It was wonderful.

She waited to see if this blanketing would continue. It did. In this sensation, she began to discern something. She saw it finally: the carsickness was the truth. A warmth and clarity pouring through her, to guide and protect her. Now making the light more clear, the air purer, the path illuminated.

She saw it all clearly now. Her view of the circumstances sharpened. The banks were done. She no longer needed them. The carsickness was the thing to keep, to stay inside of. She pitied the teller who did not have this understanding. Who would go on fixing her hair and painting her nails and smiling confusedly, without the carsickness to bring her the truth.

The truth that the dissonances were, in fact, irreconcilable.

She felt suddenly as if nothing could touch her. Like lying in Daughtry's balmy ocean, warm and sedated and enveloped tenderly. Lifted from every shard and cutting pebble below. She reached into the ostrich-skin purse and grabbed hold of the knife.

When the manager and teller returned, her voice was steady and direct.

"I have a friend outside with a gun. If you don't give me the money, he'll come inside and shoot you. If he sees you signal the guard or pick up the phone, he'll kill you."

The brunette appeared not to comprehend. She was frozen with a half smile on her face, waiting for the punch line. The manager's wall of jowls shook in fury. The waves of warmth and clearness guided B.: she had read somewhere that a bank must honor the mere threat of a weapon; she calculated that Daughtry was too far away for the manager to see his face through the glass door. She was not certain, however, if there were cameras in the parking lot.

The manager glowered at B. She knew: at her soft hair, her belling dress, her small hands.

"The ten thousand dollars now or he'll shoot," she said calmly.

The brunette's face crumpled then. There was a long pause in which B. still felt no fear, only the warm liquid clarity pouring through her. She locked eyes with the manager.

"Get the money, Cindy," he finally said.

In the car, she told Daughtry, "It's for your boat."

He held the wrapped stack of bills in disbelief. "They let you fucking go with this? Just like that?"

"You can have the boat now," she repeated.

He looked at the money, not moving.

"We should go, Harold," she told him gently.

No one followed in the side mirror yet. Daughtry was silent. They passed an orchard covered in blight, half the leaves brown and shrunken. But the sight did not disturb B. It seemed a natural part of the new gift of the carsickness, the relentless truth, the laying bare. When the Mustang was on the highway, she ducked under Daughtry's legs and rounded up the rest of the money. All of her actions clear and natural in her body without her having to understand them. She smoothed the bills into a single bundle.

"It's better if you keep everything for us," she explained, handing it to him.

He slid the bundle inside his lapel pocket mechanically. His forehead was ashen with sweat. "You're different than I thought you were," he said. "You're not the other girl at all."

It was not clearly admiration or disappointment, and B. felt she could only agree.

"I'm a little shaky," she said. "Let's drive for a while and get a bottle somewhere."

He nodded. He seemed too stunned for the moment to argue with her.

It began to fragment here. Beautifully. Her body on one side, apart, abstract. For the first time since childhood. Whether it was appealing or not, adorned or not. Her body now a vessel for the warm light of the carsickness. She thought of worrying and fretting about bare shins or chipped nails or mussed hair and she wanted to laugh.

Daughtry pulled off at a gas station with a convenience store attached. He paused after he cut the engine, put his hand on her knee.

"You okay?"

"I'm fine."

It was true. In the fragmenting, she was warm and calm and clear. She was not, anywhere in her tissue and nerves, waiting for things to work out. She watched her body in the seat, holding on.

Daughtry didn't remove his hand. She observed his worn leather cuff on her dress.

"Really. I feel better now."

He let out a sigh and moved his hand to stroke her cheek. "I'm glad, baby. I'm glad I know you like this." She watched him go into the store. The hot sun on the car felt no different than the heat all through her. The cuff of his leather blazer worn to cracks against the green poplin dress lingered in her mind. The carsickness—a boon, she was understanding now—laying the dissonances bare: Daughtry was a good man, and he would not succeed; she and he did not belong anywhere, and they did not belong together. The worn leather cuff and the green poplin dress. No one wanted to hear about her basement apartment; her mother was frightened for her; the girls would be free and bare-shinned. The blighted trees stood next to the healthy. This laying bare did not frighten her. She was not frightened.

She would only need to drive now. She would only need to keep going.

Then came another piece of clarity: he would never let her go. He would want her to stay with him, to take care of her, to put headbands in her hair and catch her fish for their soups. Her body in the fragmenting took this in.

Daughtry came back and got behind the steering wheel with a brown paper bag. "This will smooth things out. Then we'll get on the road. We can make the border by morning."

"Let's stop and drink it somewhere first."

"Naw, let's drink while we roll. Faster we get going, better I'll feel."

"I want to stop first."

He looked at her defiantly. She felt it beginning. She put on her bedroom eyes for him.

Ruth Galm

"Okay, alright. Just for a little while, baby."

From there, she heard and saw pieces in the fragmenting, from inside the carsickness. "Baby, alright, baby." Fingers at the nape of her neck. A dirt road, a wind break, leaves skimming the ground. Daughtry laying out the leather blazer once more. "Fishing boats, Mexico . . . Together. Together." The smooth sharp steel in her hand, the gash in his arm. Against the pale and black hairs the blood bubbling out. Mouth open, no words. The other hand grabbing for her, squirming, then a flick at his cheek, shallow, more blood. A moan. Moans. The eyes. The sad eyes she could not help. Dirt kicked up, sun flaring.

Back in the Mustang, keys in the ignition, wet stains on her dress.

And then: free.

IV

33.

SHE WOKE WITH A CRICK in her neck and an imprint on her cheek from the backseat of the Mustang. She had no idea how long she had driven or where she had gone, and she knew she must have stopped only from sheer exhaustion. Her throat was dry, a white mucus filmed over her lips. She tasted her own breath. Her head stung and when she reached into her hair, she found the plastic headband digging into her scalp. She cracked it in two and dropped the pieces to the floor.

Somewhere in the night she had put back on the ivory sheath. Somewhere in the night she had thrown the green poplin stained with blood out the window, had rubbed off her makeup. She did not look in the rearview mirror or at the compact but felt the smears on her cheeks. Her cuticles were grimed black.

The Mustang was hidden in trees. She faintly remembered

driving into the walnut orchard from the road. Farther and farther up the wide row into the middle. She stepped out and stood in the dust, breathing in the piquant smell of the unripe walnuts. Her body was hot with the spinning and nausea. The warm benevolent carsickness continuing to pulse through her.

She went to the trunk of the Mustang. Her body still understanding before she did what actions to take. She removed her makeup case from the travel bag and one by one tossed its contents, the eyeliner, the mascara, the lipsticks, into the dust.

In the shade of a tree, she took off the bone-colored heels and buried her toes in the dirt. Some of the hard green fruits had fallen and split, the open rinds intensifying the scent, transporting her to a faraway land. Her mind was an even plane inside the warm spinning. Why had she so resisted the truth? She braided and unbraided a strand of her hair, wondering.

When she stood up, she was unconscious of the dried mud all over the sheath, the dust and rind sap on her legs. She went back to the travel bag. The diamond brooch she laid very carefully in the dust, next to the bone-colored heels. Apart from her they were a curious still life, the significance of which seemed important.

Important but not of interest.

34.

SHE LOST TRACK OF THE hours. Several times gazing up into a walnut tree, she was dazed by the sun. This blinding seemed to bloom from the heat in her skull. In it, images came to her. The girl in the suede vest and leather anklet dancing around the circle of stars and moon, chanting, then shaking B. violently. "You should've taken it for yourself," she said. "Why didn't you just take it?"

The girl vanished before B. could answer and she was left staring at the stars and moon alone. But what was it that she had wanted? What should she have taken? She pressed her fingers into her forehead. Now all B. wanted was the carsickness. She waited for the girl to return so she could explain, but the girl did not reappear. B. rocked herself gently back and forth, humming something from *The King and I*, a tune about a dance but she could no longer remember the words.

AT SOME POINT, SHE CLEANED the knife. The blood had thickened to a gluey film. Daughtry was already out of her mind. In the end, he had nothing to do with it.

SHE WAITED UNTIL DARK TO leave. The even sharper scent of the rinds in the moonlight invigorated her, made her linger. But she knew she must move on. She walked barefoot to the car, started the engine. The headlights on the rows of trunks animated them into a momentary line of compatriots, waving her off.

She pulled in at the first gas station to fill the tank and get something to eat, but there was a police car at the pumps. She kept to the side roads after that.

35.

Darkness swallowed the valley. The black wall on either side of her total and yet incapable of penetrating the even plane in her mind. She thought she passed the chapel, a brief white flash in the road. But there was no need to try to pray now. She had everything she needed.

36.

WHEN THE SUNRISE CAME SHE did not get off the roads. On the contrary, the light refracting off the blue enamel projected her out into the valley in infinite beams of power and strength.

She wished she could tell her mother.

37.

SHE THOUGHT BRIEFLY OF THE girl from the bridge. Who must have hung in the same warm spinning. Who, as she stood out over the endless turquoise water, must have felt the certainty and precision of its truth.

IN THE BUTTES THE SUN was coming down, golden through the oak leaves, shadowed on the heavy green of the chaparral. She left the Mustang and walked up the same path. (And yet the urge to find the same tree had left her. She hoped in the end it was new.) It did not hurt her foot to climb, the wound was healed, and her bare feet never sensed the hard dirt or spiked grass going up, her body the thick air, the ostrich-skin purse swaying at her side. She sat under a tree and looked out over the valley. An inscrutable plateau of brown and green, yellow and pink. Impossible for her to imagine what was beyond the dull haze. She could not get to it.

As the moments passed, sitting with the knife, B.'s mind floated with dark, choking figures. High voices gasping for air.

She tried to talk to them, to soothe them; she tried but they only vaporized into the sun.

And then an image came that comforted her. A field she remembered, a single dead field in the midst of all the green. Yellow, desiccated husks, as if everything had been carefully grown and cultivated and then abruptly given up, left without water to shrivel and die. Now its withered limbs waiting to be torched so all could start anew.

A small breeze came up the side of the buttes, through the oak tree. B.'s hair blew loosely in the hot dry air. She did not lift her hand from the knife to fix it.

Acknowledgments

First and foremost, my deepest gratitude to Mark Doten and Bronwen Hruska. You got this book when no one else (in publishing) seemed to get it. I would not be here without the audacity of Soho Press. To Mark specifically for his brilliant eye and ear, his gift for arc and story that made the book better; you are a winning-lottery-ticket of an editor. To everyone at Soho—Abby Koski, I'm looking at you—you make dreams come true. Thank you.

To the Ucross Foundation, heaven on earth, where I found my ending.

To everyone in my life, beloved friends and family, who supported my declaration that I was writing a novel without once calling me crazy (to my face) or seeing a page of it. To Mary Gordon, whose love and friendship have been an unanticipated treasure in this life, and whose single comment opened up the whole book. To Kara Levy, Helene Wecker, Brian Eule, Zoë Ferraris, and Michael McAllister for countless infusions of moral support (and to Kara and Helene for invaluable early-draft reads). To Mary Hansen for helping me get this book into the world. To Khristina Wenzinger for generous and vital help on pacing and structure. To Ingalisa Schrobsdorff, Sheehan Grant, and Adam Cimino for being early and steadfast champions.

To Clare Beams, how do I honor the level of attention you showed this book, the meta and micro ways you nudged it into what it became. I am perpetually grateful.

To Michelle Adelman, words are inadequate. For your sanity and communion in writing, book drafts, and living life. To Emilee Yawn, for friendship and creative kinship beyond imagining.

To Bernard Galm, literary co-enthusiast and devoted uncle. To Stacey Berg, for planting a seed for the novel, encouraging its most embryonic form, and for unwavering love and encouragement. To Amalia, Ella, and Ruby Galm for being the best-ever antidote to writing.

And finally, to Paul Galm. For an almost inexhaustible capacity to walk with me through the days, for the love, humor, and real talk that make me the luckiest sister I could imagine.